EastEnders

Steve Owen: STILL WATERS

Kate Lock

This book is published to accompany the television series *EastEnders*.

BBC Controller, Drama Series: Mal Young
Executive Producer: John Yorke

Published by BBC Worldwide Ltd, 80 Wood Lane, London W12 0TT

First published 2001

ISBN 0 563 53722 1

Commissioning Editor: Emma Shackleton
Project Editors: Helena Caldon and Rhianwen Bailey
Copy Editor: Barbara Nash
Editorial Consultants: Robert Perry and Sharon Batten

Typeset in Sabon and Compacta by BBC Worldwide Ltd
Printed and bound in Great Britain by MacKays of Chatham
Colour separations by Radstock Reproductions Ltd, Midsomer Norton
Colour section printed by Lawrence Allen Ltd, Weston-super-Mare
Cover printed by Belmont Press Ltd, Northampton

THE AUTHOR

Kate Lock was born in Oxford and began her career as a journalist on the *Oxford Star*. She has written extensively about television for *Radio Times* and has published seven TV novelisations and one non-fiction book.

Other books by Kate Lock:

Where the Heart Is: Home
Where the Heart Is: Relative Values
EastEnders: Blood Ties – The Life and Loves of Grant Mitchell
Tiffany's Secret Diary
Bianca's Secret Diary
Who's Who in EastEnders

Writing as K M Lock:

Jimmy McGovern's The Lakes
Burnside: The Secret Files

WALFORD WEDDING SHOOTING

A Walford man was shot on his doorstep yesterday as unknowing local residents celebrated a wedding only a few yards away. Garage owner and local businessman Phil Mitchell was shot at close range when he answered the door to his house in Albert Square. No witnesses to the crime have as yet come forward and a motive for the shooting is unclear.

He was discovered unconscious and lying in a pool of blood by neighbour Beppe di Marco, best man at the wedding of nightclub owner Steve Owen and Melanie Beale, which was being celebrated at the nearby Queen Victoria pub. Mr di Marco, a former policeman, performed CPR on him, which, according to GP Dr Anthony Trueman, who attended the scene, almost certainly saved his life. Mr Mitchell was rushed to hospital, where an emergency operation was performed to remove the bullet. His condition was today described as 'critical'.

Phil Mitchell, the owner of Mitchell's Auto Repairs, has several other business interests in Walford, inlcuding a limo service, café and snooker hall. He is generally considered to be a shrewd, hard-working teetotaller who commands respect in the community, although one local, who wished to remain anonymous, said that he had in recent months 'upset half of Albert Square'. Police are continuing to interview local residents, but no arrests have so far been made. A spokesman said he expected the process to take 'some time'. When asked why, he said that they were pursuing multiple leads, but refused to be drawn further.

In the hours leading up to the shooting, Phil Mitchell had attended the wedding reception at nightclub E20 along with most of the other Albert Square residents. He left early after in a heated discussion with the bride, Melanie Owen, and Ian Beale, her ex-husband. The altercation between Mr Mitchell and Mr Beale, which continued outside the nightclub was witnessed by local stallholder Mark Fowler and Mitchell's former girlfriend Lisa Shaw. Mr Fowler described the victim as 'abusive'. Miss Shaw was too distressed to comment.

The bride and groom left for a honeymoon in the Caribbean shortly after the incident. Steve Owen, who runs the Turpin Road nightclub, has achieved local notoriety himself, having two years ago been acquitted of the murder of his ex-girlfriend, Saskia Duncan. Matthew Rose, who worked as a DJ for Steve Owen, was found guilty of manslaughter, but was later released from prison after new evidence was discovered. Miss Duncan was killed with a blow to the head from a heavy ashtray and her body was buried in Epping Forest.

Walford Gazette 2 March 2001

ONE

'Congratulations, Mr Owen. Mrs Owen.' The unfamiliar name took a moment to register. Mel looked up and saw a stewardess standing in front of them with champagne. The stewardess bestowed a dazzling, premium-cabin smile through a mask of make-up. 'Please accept this with our compliments. On behalf of the captain and crew, I'd like to wish you a very happy honeymoon.'

Steve glanced at the label. 'Nice one.' He squeezed Mel's hand. 'Start as we mean to go on, eh?'

'I'll drink to that.' She accepted a fizzing glass.

'To new beginnings,' he said, smiling broadly.

'New beginnings,' she repeated, her own smile less confident. He saluted her with his glass, holding her eyes as he drank. Mel wondered if he was being ironic. Sometimes, it was difficult to tell with Steve. He was so good at putting on an act. She had been unable to gauge his real feelings since the wedding yesterday. Considering that he'd found out about her dirty little secret, he had been remarkably restrained. She had been stunned when, after stumbling guiltily through her vows, Steve had kissed her and whispered significantly that he 'knew'. Her heart had plummeted. Suddenly, it had all made sense. That was why he had been so off-hand with her the other night in the club. Phil must have told Steve himself, she guessed, though she couldn't work out when he'd had the opportunity. On the way back from the registry office she had tried to get Steve to talk, but he had made it clear that he did not want to discuss it. For a split second his eyes had flared a warning, and then he'd switched on a sociable smile for the waiting guests and taken her arm possessively. Mel had expected fireworks – a row, a fight, on-the-spot annulment. Of all the reactions she had anticipated, a show of marital harmony wasn't one of them. Particularly when it had continued in private. It was unnerving.

Only this morning at their Heathrow hotel she had again tried to bring the subject up, but Steve had told her to forget about it and concentrate on their future. If only it was that easy, she thought, looking out of the plane window. Steve was not the type to forgive, or forget. When she had pressed him, he had got angry and said it was all sorted. Phil, he had ranted, was history. If this was intended to reassure her, it only served to make Mel more nervous. Steve and Phil had already come to blows over the business with E20, and the vein of hatred between them ran deep. Not that she felt any less bitter towards Phil for the calculated and callous way he'd treated her and, more specifically, poor, pregnant Lisa. The man deserved all he got. He was twisted and dangerous and a thoroughly nasty piece of work. She didn't care what happened to Phil; she just didn't want Steve mixed up in any reprisals. It would only lead to more bad blood and poison their marriage. Better to end it here and now, draw a line under the whole thing. Otherwise, who knew what the outcome might be? Steve had killed before. Didn't they say the first time was the hardest? What if he had less scruples about getting rid of Phil? Saskia's death had been an accident, but not even Steve could get away with murder twice.

Mel shuddered. You're letting your imagination run away with you, she scolded herself. Steve rubbed her arm solicitously. 'Want me to get you a blanket?' He reached for the call button.

'No, it's alright, I'm not cold.'

'Someone step on your grave, did they?'

'I hate that saying. It's so creepy. Makes me imagine...' her voice petered out.

'When your number's up, your number's up.' He drained his glass. 'No point in worrying about it. The thing is to get on and enjoy life. Refill?'

'I'm fine, thanks.' Mel took another sip. Peering at him over the rim of her glass, she said, 'So you believe it's all down to fate, do you?'

'The great bingo-caller in the sky?' He laughed mirthlessly. 'I believe we have choices, Mel. If I get a gun and shoot someone, that isn't destiny, that's deliberate.'

Mel flinched. Given Steve's history, his remark was at best inappropriate. At worst, it confirmed what she'd just been thinking, and she wasn't going to go there. 'I see,' she said lightly, deflecting the implication with an attempt at humour. 'Remind me never to annoy you.'

'I'm just saying, that's how it works.'

'And that's Steve Owen's philosophy, is it?'

'Not literally. That was just an example.'

'Oh, good. Because otherwise I was going to ask them to turn the plane round and fly me home.'

'Too late for that.' He put his arm around her shoulders and kissed her, a lingering, champagne-flavoured snog. 'I've got you now.'

'Mmm.'

She snuggled up to him, resting her head on his chest. Better to keep quiet about Phil, she decided. Steve didn't seem to blame her, and that was the main thing. The past couple of months had been hell, worrying about it. All in all, she had been very lucky; there were surely few new spouses who would be that understanding. What was important now was to move on, as Steve had said, and a fortnight in the Caribbean was just what they needed to take their minds off it. There would be plenty of time to face up to the consequences when they were back in Walford.

'If you look out to your left, that's the Dominican Republic below us now.' The captain's commentary broke into Mel's dreams. She rubbed her eyes, regretting the champagne – it had been so good, they had ordered another bottle – which had left her with a parched mouth and thumping headache. Why hadn't she followed all those magazine tips about sticking to water? Peeling her tongue off the roof of her mouth, she signalled to the still-immaculate stewardess, who brought tea and hot lemon-scented flannels. Mel buried her face in one, comforted by the heat. Beside her, Steve stretched and yawned. 'Where are we?'

'Flying over the West Indies.'

'Not long now, then.' He leaned over and kissed her on the cheek. 'Good morning.'

'Is it? I've lost all track of time.'

'Yeah, well, it's best to stick to your own body clock, adjust gradually.' He glanced at his watch. 'Imagine you're just bringing the milk in.'

Mel pictured herself in dressing-gown and slippers, picking up the gritty milk bottles off the front step, hearing the shouts of market traders and the rattle of Underground trains. Albert Square seemed a million miles away. She wondered how Lisa was coping. Their friendship meant a great deal to her, and, having just mended it after the rift over Phil, Mel felt a pang of guilt at not being there to support her in her vulnerable state. Still, at least Lisa had Mark, she consoled herself. He seemed willing to fight her corner. She fumbled in her bag for a hairbrush and began brushing her long hair energetically, creating crackles of static electricity.

'Carry on like that and you'll trip the mains,' Steve joked.

She shook her hair back, tying it up in a ponytail, and started to massage moisturizer into her dehydrated skin with unnecessary vigour. He studied her pink and rather shiny face. 'Everything all right?'

'Sure. Why shouldn't it be?'

'You seem a bit agitated.'

'Just thinking about Lisa.' She patted on eye gel, pulling a face at herself in a hand mirror. 'God, I look knackered.'

'You've had a lot on your plate. Weddings are stressful times – they're up in the top three with bereavement and moving house.'

'Well, that's two out of three, then.'

He gave a short laugh. 'You ain't even moved in, yet. Now, forget about Walford, and Lisa, and whatever else you're worrying about and start thinking about Jamaica. In a few hours time you'll be stretched out on a white beach under a palm tree with a cocktail at your elbow and your own personal manservant to rub your sun cream in.' He flexed his fingers, grinning.

'I'll hold you to that.'

'You'll like it. I'm very thorough.' She felt herself melting with the promise. Steve gazed at her smokily. 'Though I'm not sure I can wait that long. Fancy making this marriage official?'

'I seem to remember we did that last night. And this morning.'

'Might as well go for the hat-trick, then.'

'You mean...?' Mel nodded at the loo. 'Don't they have monitors or something?'

'That's to catch smokers.' He leaned over and whispered in her ear. Mel put her hand over her mouth to silence her snort of laughter. 'Absolutely not.'

'And I thought you were the adventurous type. Remember the carousel at Brighton?' Steve stood up, stretching his legs. He winked at her. 'You're not going to go all safe and boring on me now, are you?'

Mel drew a deep breath. 'You go ahead. I'll just get my, er, toothbrush.'

Over breakfast, Mel quizzed Steve about their destination. 'Tell me more about this place. I don't even know which part of Jamaica we're going to. You've been very secretive about it.'

'Wait and see.' He forked in scrambled eggs and smoked salmon hungrily.

'Come on, Steve,' Mel pleaded. 'You can tell me now. Please.'

'I love it when you beg.' He paused to butter a toasted muffin and tore into it with white teeth.

'Steve!'

'All right. It's near Montego Bay.'

'Is that all you're going to tell me?'

He appeared to consider this carefully. 'Yes.'

Mel looked out at the blue expanse of the Caribbean twinkling below them in the bright sunlight. The plane had started its slow descent towards Jamaica and she could just make out the dots of fishing vessels and the white crests of waves.

'So how did you find out about this place – travel company or Internet? Barry says you can get some great deals on-line.'

'Unless your name's Terry Raymond.'

Mel giggled. 'Yeah, I hope you read the small print.'

'No.'

'Steve! You might have committed us to anything.'

'Don't worry, I got it through a mate. Top notch. Everything's been arranged for us.'

Mel's heart sank. 'This isn't something dodgy, is it?'

'Would I do that to you?' He drained his coffee cup and gestured to the stewardess for a refill.

Mel put down her croissant. Suddenly, she had lost her appetite. 'I don't know, Steve. I really don't know.'

The first thing that hit them when they disembarked at Sangster International Airport was the humidity. The warm, thick air seemed to fill their lungs like soup. Sweating on the scorching tarmac, Steve donned shades and took Mel's hand. 'Let's get out of here,' he shouted over the roar of the jet engines.

They hurried inside the air-conditioned terminal building. After passing through immigration, they reclaimed their luggage and were waved through customs and into the arrivals hall. A man in a smart grey uniform was waiting for them, holding up the name 'Owen' on a piece of cardboard.

'There's our driver,' Steve said, looking pleased.

They followed the man – who introduced himself as Benny – outside, bypassing a queue of taxis blaring soca and reggae. Benny led them to a huge silver Mercedes and opened the door for Mel with a courtly gesture. She flopped on to the leather seats, grateful for the car's temperature-regulated interior. Steve slipped in on the other side, giving her a grin.

'This is the way to travel, eh?' He squeezed her hand. 'First class all the way. Nothing but the best for my wife.'

Mel regarded him curiously. 'That's the first time you've called me that.'

'Is it?'

'Yes. I rather like it.' She leaned over and kissed him softly on the lips. Drawing back, she caught Steve looking at her almost wonderingly, as if he couldn't believe his luck.

The big saloon took off smoothly and accelerated on to the coast road heading eastwards out of Montego Bay. Gliding past luxury resorts, stately plantation-style villas and manicured golf courses, even laid-back Steve seemed impressed. Mel, almost dizzy with the riot of hot colours and the lush foliage, was for once speechless.

'You like Mobay?' Benny gesticulated at the azure sea, which was criss-crossed with the foam trails of jet skis and powerboats.

'Sorry?'

'Mo Bay,' he repeated, pronouncing the two words separately. 'That's what we call it. Playground of the rich an' famous.' He winked at Steve in the driver's mirror. Steve's lips twitched.

'It's beautiful,' Mel breathed, staring out at the water.

Far below them, white yacht sails like butterfly wings fluttered in the brisk off-shore breeze. A parachute puffed out from the sea, rising like a cloud and taking someone para-ascending high into the sky behind a speedboat.

'See the ship?' Benny was keen to give them the guided tour. 'Mobay gets many cruise ships. The passengers spend a lotta money.' He rubbed his fingers together, laughing.

They looked back at the port, which dominated the old town below, and saw a hulking cruise ship tied up in a massive berth. Another was visible on the horizon.

'Better than Kingston. The people here are real nice. Except for them rass higglers. You watch out for them.'

It was hard at times to make out his Jamaican patois, though from the invective it was clear that 'rass' was not a compliment.

'Higglers?' Steve queried.

'Down at the port. Ask you for money. Sell you ganja.' He clicked his tongue, shaking his head. 'No good for Mobay. This the Friendly City. Like me.'

Benny looked back over the seat at them, grinning. Mel wished he would keep his eyes on the road.

'You drive on the left here.' Tactfully, Steve brought Benny's attention back to his driving.

'British system.' He laughed. 'Home from home for you.'

Steve turned to Mel. 'Speaking of which... I think we're almost there. Is this it, Benny?'

'Comin' up on the left, Mr Owen.'

Steve dug in his pocket and brought out a large cotton handkerchief. 'Shut your eyes,' he ordered Mel.

'Hey. I'll look like a kidnap victim if I roll up with this on,' she resisted.

'Come on, Mel. It's all part of the surprise.'

'I must be mad,' she grumbled, letting him tie the blindfold on her.

The car slowed, swinging into a driveway under a sign reading 'Crescent Beach Club', then continued through landscaped parkland. She felt it scrunch over gravel and come to a halt.

'Stay here a minute,' Steve ordered. 'And no looking.'

She heard the door slam and footsteps retreating. A minute passed. Mel, feeling conspicuous, was about to yank the blindfold off when Steve came bounding back. He flung open the car door and helped her out. A gentle breeze caressed her, lifting her hair and wrapping her skirt around her legs. She breathed in the fragrant scent of blossoms, felt the warmth of the sun on her skin, and smiled. 'Lead on, then.'

Steve took her hand. 'We're through here. Watch your step.'

She felt grass beneath her feet. The sound of the sea was becoming louder, surf swelling and crashing rhythmically followed by the sigh of the backwash. A seabird cried plaintively. In the distance, the strains of calypso mingled with the shrieks and calls of bathers. Steve steadied her along a path and guided her up a small flight of steps, then stopped. She felt him fumble with the knot of the hankie and pushed it up herself impatiently. Ahead of her was a gracious white Georgian villa standing in its own private garden, looking out across a crescent-shaped bay of pure white sand fringed with coconut palms. Mel turned to Steve, tears in her eyes.

'Does that mean you like it or you hate it?' he asked, smudging away a tear with his thumb.

'I love it.' She flung her arms around him. 'And I love you, too.'

'You had me worried there for a second.'

He nuzzled her neck, stroking her hair. Mel relaxed against him, feeling all the tension of the past few weeks flowing out of her.

'Right, hold on tight.' So saying, Steve bent and scooped her up. Mel shrieked with laughter as he pushed open the door and carried her over the threshold. He put her down in a cool, high, tiled hallway crammed with arrangements of fresh flowers. 'Welcome to paradise.'

Not only was the villa equipped and decorated to the standard of a mini-mansion, it also had its own pool. Mel and Steve were inspecting this when there was a chink of ice behind them. They looked round to see a pretty girl in a white apron and oddly old-fashioned mob cap. She was bearing a silver tray on which stood a large jug festooned with fruit.

'Good day to you.' She chanted it parrot-fashion, then smiled shyly. 'Me Serena, the maid.' She placed the tray on a poolside table, which was sheltered from the midday sun by a shady umbrella. 'Would you like a cocktail now?'

'Ooh, yes please,' Mel said, taking a seat. 'What is it?'

'Rum punch. The traditional drink of Jamaica.'

'I mix cocktails at the pub where I work.' Mel watched as Serena poured two tall glasses. 'What's in it?'

'Light rum, pineapple juice, orange juice, lime juice, red syrup – and overproof rum.'

'That's pretty lethal stuff,' Steve said.

Serena giggled. 'Drink this and you won't be walkin' far today.'

'We weren't planning on going anywhere – were we?' Steve interjected, grinning at Mel.

She smiled back. 'Just crashing out, I should think.'

'You on honeymoon, yes?' Serena winked at Steve. 'I will get cook to fix you a special drink, keep you ... strong.'

Steve's grin faded. Mel kept an admirably straight face. 'What's that, Serena? Sounds like it would go down a bomb at the Vic.'

'Mauby. It's a tree bark. In Jamaica, all the men drink it. Women, too. If you want to get ... ' She gestured a pregnant belly.

'So it's an aphrodisiac?'

'It's a *love* potion,' she drawled.

'What does it taste like?'

Serena pulled a face.

'That bad?' Mel laughed.

'But afterward, you won't be complainin'.'

The two women cackled uproariously. Shaking his head, Steve took a large draught of punch. Gasping, he spluttered, 'I think I'll stick with this.'

After a delicious lunch of peppered shrimp and marlin steaks, prepared by their personal cook, Dolly, even the infamous mauby would have been hard-pressed to have an effect. Mel and Steve, who had polished off the jug of punch and washed down lunch with Red Stripes, could do no more than stagger into their luxurious bedroom and collapse on the four-poster in a sozzled tangle.

When they awoke the sun was sinking into the sea, streaking the sky with a palette of pink and purple, red and gold. Mel, standing by the open window in a silk slip, felt a strange kind of peace descend on her. She closed her eyes, letting the balmy breeze fan her cheek, and rested her head on the wood of the window frame. The evening orchestra of crickets and frogs was tuning up, unfamiliar birds twittering from the trees darkening against the lurid sky. Time, which usually rushed by too fast, seemed to have slowed to a different pace.

'Happy?'

Mel felt a kiss on her bare shoulder and looked up to see Steve, naked except for a white towel wrapped round his waist, sarong-style. His body was still damp from the shower and he had tiny droplets clinging to his chest hair. He pulled her against him and she buried her face in his warm musky skin.

'Blissfully,' she murmured.

He lifted her chin and gazed into her eyes. 'You are so beautiful, you know that?' He stroked her lips with his thumb. 'Every man who sees you, wants you. And I'm the one that's got you. I'm a lucky man.' He bent his head to kiss her, a hard hungry kiss, before taking her by the hand and leading her back to the bed.

Strolling along the moonlit beach later, neither Steve nor Mel had ever seen stars so big and bright.

'I can't get over how close they look,' Mel said, tipping her face to the sky. 'You almost feel you can reach out and touch them.'

The sound of laughter drifted out from the gaily lit main house, a short distance back, which was full of diners enjoying a cabaret. The old plantation house, which had been carved up into de luxe rooms and suites, comprised the main part of the exclusive resort. The handsome villas, of which there were twenty, occupied the prime position along the waterfront and were clearly the most expensive.

'Who owns this place? It's not a chain, is it?' Mel asked, listening to the strains of music.

'A bloke called Taylor. Multimillionaire.'

'Do you know him?'

'Not personally.'

'Only, I was wondering ... ' She paused, trying to find the right words. ' ... I mean, it's obviously pretty ritzy. Some of the people up in the bar earlier, they had bodyguards. And I swear that woman in the low-cut silver gown was a Hollywood actress. I know I've seen her in something.' She stopped walking and turned to Steve. 'We're talking serious money here, aren't we?'

'It's not cheap. But you're worth every penny.'

'Come on. This is thousands. I know E20's going well, but you've just bought out Beppe. You can't be that flush.'

'The club's doing OK. There's no need to worry.'

'I'm not stupid, Steve,' she retorted. 'So don't pat me on the head and tell me it's not my business. I married you. It is my business.'

He was silent, his face impossible to read in the dark. Mel felt a surge of anger. 'What have you got us into, Steve? I asked you on the plane if it was something dodgy and you didn't give me a straight answer then.' She took a shaky breath. 'Well, I want one now.'

TWO

'It's a wedding present. From a mate of mine.' Steve shrugged. 'Look, it's no big deal, Mel. I'm not about to bankrupt us. All I had to fork out for was the flights.'

She studied him suspiciously. 'Some mate of yours shells out an arm and a leg for your honeymoon? Must be a very good friend.'

'He is.'

'So why haven't I met this secret benefactor of yours?'

'He lives in Spain.' Steve put his arm around Mel's shoulders. 'Come on, let's go and get a nightcap.'

'No. I'm not moving until you tell me all about this bloke.' Mel sat down on the sand. 'You know I won't be able to relax and enjoy myself if you keep it some big mystery. I'll be imagining all sorts. So, spill.'

'Ever heard the saying about not looking a gift horse in the mouth?' He flopped down beside her. 'I didn't know you were so cynical, Mel.'

She shot him a sidewards look. 'I can't believe you, of all people, just said that.'

'All right, all right.' He grinned weakly. 'But there's nothing dodgy about it. I've checked it all out thoroughly.'

'Go on.'

Steve leaned back, propping himself on his elbows, and stretched his long legs out in front of him. Looking out to sea, he continued, 'I used to work for this geezer down in Dover, Tony Sheen. Took me on as a bar manager in this nightclub. Champers, it was called.' He chuckled. 'I was twenty-two, cocky as hell, thought I knew it all. He knocked some sense into me, taught me the business.'

'Cocky, you? I'd never have guessed.'

'Yeah, well, I soon wised up, learned when to throw my weight around, when to keep my mouth shut. Tony could see I had potential. We were on the same wavelength, even though he was quite a lot older than me. It was a good partnership.'

'So what happened?'

'A couple of years later, Tony moved on to a new club in

Romford. He hadn't been running it for long when he got another opportunity. He suggested I take over from him and two weeks later I was managing my own club.'

'How did you get on, being thrown in the deep end?'

'I did a bloody good job.' He grinned at her. 'It was the best night spot around.'

'Says who?' she teased.

'It wasn't some grotty little dive. I had top acts, top DJs ... people came from miles away. It was a classy set-up.'

'Not the ten-lagers-a-curry-and-a-fight sort of place?'

'We had our share of troublemakers.' He picked up a handful of sand, letting it trickle through his fingers. 'You always do with clubs; goes with the territory. I stepped up security, knocked it on the head.'

Mel hugged her knees. 'How long were you there for?'

'I ran it for seven years. After that, Tony decided he was retiring and put the club on the market. He had all sorts of operations on the go by then and his wife was giving him grief about never seeing him. He had this villa in Spain and decided to live out his years in Puerto Banus watching the yachts come in.'

'And the club?'

'He sold it for a packet, along with the other clubs. There was no way I could afford that kind of money, he knew that, so he offered me the leasehold on this West End joint of his, dirt cheap. He practically gave it to me. Said it was a leaving present.' Steve rolled over on to his stomach. 'That was when I met Saskia.'

Mel could not see his face. She sensed this was intentional. Steve never talked about Saskia and she didn't like to push it. Not yet.

'So you've stayed in touch with this Tony, then?' she asked lightly.

'On and off. He popped back a few times, saw the changes I'd made to the club. I went over to Spain myself and stayed with him. I haven't heard much from him recently. That was why I got in contact with him again. I thought he might come to the wedding.'

Mel bit her lip. Neither of their families had been well represented at the wedding. Both her parents had produced convenient excuses, a fact that had rankled with her although Steve hadn't cared. Jackie's excuses had been equally flimsy, but Mel suspected it had more to do with Steve's choice of best man. After her treatment of Gianni, Jackie was unpopular with the di Marcos, and Beppe was nothing if not loyal to his brother. Steve had been philosophical about his sister's no-show, but his shuttered face had betrayed disappointment. Steve and Jackie were close, unlike Steve and his mother. Barbara Owen had not been invited – 'She's too ill', Steve had said curtly, when Mel had suggested it – but had turned up anyway, having prised the details out of Billy. Steve had tensed at the sight of her and, although Mel had tried to be friendly, Barbara had remained aloof. The woman was obviously a stirrer, Mel thought. Not only had she immediately formed an alliance with Phil, she had also been snippy about her job as a barmaid, hinting that her son had married beneath him. Steve, too, had been visibly wound up by something she'd said, although he wouldn't elaborate. There was obviously a difficult history there, Mel reflected. Given that, his relationship with Tony Sheen probably meant more to Steve than he was letting on. Mel was touched.

'But he couldn't come?' she probed gently.

'Nah. He wanted to, but his wife's ill. He said he'd make it up to me, but I told him it didn't matter. Then, a week later, he called me, said had I booked the honeymoon? I told him I'd booked a package to St Kitts but you'd torn up the tickets.' He flicked sand at Mel, who pulled a face. 'Then he said, "Well, see if she'll go for a fortnight at Desmond's Taylor's swanky resort in Jamaica, cos it's all arranged".'

'It wasn't the tickets, it was just the confirmation letter,' Mel corrected him.

'Yeah, well, I got the message loud and clear.'

'So... when did you cancel St Kitts?' she dug.

'When I got offered a free honeymoon, of course. You don't think I gave up just because you threw a wobbly in the Vic, do you?' he said sardonically. 'I knew you'd come round, in the end.'

'Did you, now?' She raised an eyebrow. 'So why the charade with Kat Slater? You must have been getting *really* desperate by then.'

'Had to hurry things up a bit, didn't I? The wedding date was coming up and you were still being pig-headed.'

'Did it ever cross your mind that being less arrogant and pig-headed yourself might have worked?'

He grinned. 'Where's the fun in that?'

She hit him playfully. 'You've got a viscous streak, you have.'

'You love me for it.'

'I love you despite it. There's a difference. And that's only because I know there's another Steve underneath. A Steve capable of real, strong emotions, not just an artful manipulator.'

'Emotions? You know we men won't admit to having those'.

'I won't spread it.' She snuggled up against him, sliding her hand inside his shirt. 'You're obviously very fond of Tony, for example. Why didn't you just tell me all of this?'

'Because I couldn't afford to risk you tearing up any more tickets. Do you know how much these flights cost?' He sat up and then pounced on her unexpectedly, straddling her and pinning her down by her arms.

'Ow.' Mel pretended to struggle, but not very hard.

He held her tighter. 'And because I knew you'd go off the way you just did, spitting sparks like a Catherine wheel before I could explain.'

'Ow, ow!' This time she wasn't pretending.

'You've gotta learn to control that impulsive nature of yours, Melanie.' His eyes were dark, unsmiling. She swallowed, her mouth suddenly dry. Was he referring to her having sex with Phil? She couldn't help feeling she had got off lightly – too lightly. While the subject remained closed between them, there was still a background level of anxiety on Mel's part. It seemed inevitable there was more to come.

Steve was breathing hard, his body pressing down on hers. 'Otherwise,' he whispered, his lips brushing her ear, 'I'll have to punish you.'

Adrenalin pumped through her veins. 'How?' she challenged, brazening him out.

Without answering, he released her wrists and slid his hands slowly up her bare arms, until he was holding her by the shoulders. Mel arched her spine, ready to react.

'Like this!' he hissed, suddenly tickling her mercilessly under the arms.

Mel shrieked, rolling this way and that, her laughter more than a little wild. 'Steve! Lemme go! Steve!' She tried to crawl away, but he tackled her and dragged her back towards him.

'You're not escaping that easily.' He commenced tickling

again with hard relentless fingers.

Mel, panting, protested, 'Enough! You've ruined my dress and I've got sand in my knickers.'

He grinned wolfishly. 'Oh yeah?'

When they returned to the villa, the bedding had been turned down and fresh petals had been strewn on the crisp white linen sheets. Two presents, artistically gift-wrapped, had been placed on their pillows. On the table next to the bed, a cut-glass decanter of cognac had been set out on a tray, together with a box of handmade truffles. Propped up against the fine crystal was a card in a stiff cream envelope.

Steve opened it and read aloud, '"Welcome, honeymooners".'

'Ugh,' Mel interrupted, lacing her arms around his waist. 'I hate being called that. It's so naff.'

Looking over his shoulder she read, *Hope everything is to your satisfaction. If you need anything, don't hesitate to ask for me personally. Any friend of Tony's is a friend of mine. Regards, Desmond Taylor*. She looked up at Steve with a grin. 'Do you think he *personally* scattered the petals? Maybe we should check he isn't going to leap out of the wardrobe and serenade us with Bali Hi.' She exploded into giggles. 'Is this all included in the honeymoon package, or are we getting special treatment?'

Steve frowned fleetingly. Mel, who was tearing into her present, did not notice. 'It'll be standard practice,' he said. 'All the little extras, that's how they hike up the rates. You pay through the nose for these things.'

'Well, you're not paying through the nose for anything.' Mel held up a bottle of expensive perfume. 'In fact, your nose is in for a treat. I'm going to smell divine. Can I open yours? I bet it's cologne. No, it can't be. It rattles.' She ripped off the paper. 'Nice box. Feels a bit light.' She passed it to Steve. 'I think I've got the better deal. This stuff's really hard to get hold of.' She dabbed perfume on her wrist and sniffed. 'Mmm.' Steve was silent. Mel looked up to see him dangling a set of car keys in his hand. 'Wow. I take it all back. You win. What's the make?'

He examined the fob. 'Can't tell.'

'Hang on, let me find the label.' She scrabbled through the discarded wrapping paper. '*To Steve. For the duration. Have fun. DT.*' She raised an eyebrow. 'This generosity is a bit over the top.

What was it between you and Tony, Steve? Are you sure you've told me everything?'

Steve poured them both a generous splash of brandy and sat down on the bed next to her. 'Pretty much,' he said.

The following morning, Steve went up to the hotel car park to claim his mystery vehicle while Mel floated languorously in the pool on an inflatable sunbed. The time alone gave her an opportunity to reflect on the previous evening, on the weird intense side of Steve that he usually kept hidden from her. There had been an occasion before the wedding, when he had grilled her about Phil, when she had felt intimidated by the look in his eyes. Such moments were rare, though. That he could be cold, ruthless, frightening, Mel had no doubt. He had made Matthew bury Saskia in Epping Forest and then pressurized him into keeping silent, which took a power beyond most people. At the trial, Steve had claimed that he'd panicked. That much, Mel could believe. What he had done to enforce his hold over Matt, she didn't like to think about.

She chided herself for having been scared, however momentarily. OK, Steve had acquired a reputation over Saskia, but he was no monster – far from it. He'd risked his own life saving Jackie and Gianni from the wreck of the Arches. He had found Steven Beale when he got lost. He had been a friend to her throughout the agonizing period when she'd thought Lucy had cancer. He hadn't (unlike Phil) attempted to sabotage her wedding to Ian, even though he could have done so. In fact, he had wished her well. And afterwards, when she had been about to run away from Walford, it was Steve who had given her a bolt-hole and persuaded her to stay and face the music. He had even got Dan off her back when he was stalking her. If she needed proof of how Steve felt about her, he had already demonstrated it amply – just as he had demonstrated to her last night, on the beach.

Mel felt her stomach dip, remembering. Their lovemaking had never been so intimate. It was almost as if, by opening up about his past, Steve had shed a layer, become more transparent. He could be so shut off from her at times – it was always hard to know what he was thinking – but after last night she felt as if she was finally making inroads into the real Steve Owen. It would take a long time, but she was determined to unpick all the layers, one by one. All it needed was a little gentle coaxing. They had a fortnight of sun, sea and sand; the perfect ingredients for unwinding and learning about each other.

She shifted on the lilo, trailing a hand in the water, regretting for the hundredth time her momentary lapse with Phil Mitchell. She felt so close to Steve now, and the betrayal cut all the deeper. Still, she thought defensively, it was partly Steve's fault, wasn't it? Deep down, he must have realized that. If he hadn't been so nasty to her over the E20 thing, she wouldn't have ended up taking comfort in Phil's arms. Plus, Steve had deserted her over Christmas. Christmas, when loving couples were supposed to be together! The way things had been left, she hadn't even been sure if they had a future together. It was no wonder she'd been so confused and upset ...

A car horn sounded from the private road that ran past the villas, jolting her out of her musings. She paddled the inflatable to the side and got out, curious to see the car Desmond Taylor had loaned them. Going over to the white picket fence that surrounded 'their' property, she found Steve behind the wheel of an open-top Jeep. He looked extremely pleased with himself.

'I've always fancied an off-roader.' He revved the engine experimentally. 'It's just what we need for exploring the Blue Mountains.'

'I was planning on lying in the sun and topping up my tan, actually.'

'Yeah, well, you'll soon get bored with that.' He switched on the radio, blasting her with reggae.

She put her hands over her ears. 'For Christ's sake, turn it off, Steve. Come and have some coffee, Dolly's just made it. You can get your taste of the Blue Mountains that way.'

'OK, OK. We'll take it for a spin later. I'll take you out to one of those plantation-house restaurants for lunch. How about that?'

'Sounds good.'

They took breakfast by the pool, served by the redoubtable Dolly. Dolly, a middle-aged woman of vast proportions, had a robust sense of humour that remained undented by the trials and tribulations her large and apparently feckless family regularly put her through. (Mel and Steve had already had Dolly's life story, which had been served up in instalments with the previous day's lunch.)

'I could get used to this.' Mel stretched out her arms, yawning lazily. 'Nothing to do but be waited on hand and foot. I feel like royalty.' She watched as an iridescent hummingbird hovered in front of a mango flower, inserting its long thin beak to extract the nectar. 'Look, Steve, see that bird?'

'That's a doctor bird,' said Dolly, reappearing with freshly baked rolls.

Steve, however, paid no attention to the bird. He was observing the gardener on the adjacent plot, who had been clipping the same bush for the past ten minutes. 'Who's that?' he asked.

Dolly craned her neck. 'That Francis. Him work for Mr Taylor.' She leaned towards Mel and hissed, 'Him come around here yesterday, asking me this an' that. Yabbering worse than a woman! Vex me proper.'

'Maybe he likes you,' Mel suggested.

'Cho!' Dolly snorted. 'And maybe him don't want to do no work.'

Mel buttered a warm roll and passed it to Steve. 'Try this, it's fantastic.'

'No, thanks.' Steve got to his feet. 'I'm just going up to the big house, get some leaflets on places to visit. You take your time. I'll be back soon.' So saying, he left, striding away purposefully. Mel, taken aback, watched him go.

Dolly shook her head disapprovingly. 'Mr Steve need to ease up.'

'I agree, Dolly. He just hasn't got acclimatized to the Jamaican way of things yet. It takes a bit of adjusting when you're used to the pace of London life.' Mel wriggled her bare toes. 'Not that I'm having any problems.'

She shut her eyes and lay back on her sunlounger, listening to the regular slap and hiss of the surf. Apart from the squawk of a parrot, the little garden was peaceful. Even the snip-snip-snip of next door's hedge clippers had ceased.

By the time Steve had slipped round the back of his neighbour's garden, Francis had disappeared. Steve wasn't entirely surprised; he'd had a feeling about the man since they arrived. It wasn't anything he could put his finger on, exactly; rather the fact that Francis seemed to have cropped up once too often in the space of twenty-four hours. First he had been deputized to carry their luggage, then he had appeared again (albeit disguised with a baseball cap and baggy overalls) to rake the lawn in front of the villa. It had seemed to Steve, whose sharp eyes noticed details like this, an odd combination of jobs. Either the guy was a porter or a gardener, surely? His suspicions were compounded when he took delivery of the Jeep and spotted Francis assiduously polishing a black BMW on the other side of the hotel car park. Seeing him back in his gardening togs loitering in the shrubbery was pushing credibility to its limit, and Dolly's remark about his visit to the house had been the final clincher. Francis was obviously spying on them.

Steve hadn't said anything to Mel – he didn't want to alarm her unduly – but his nose for trouble was definitely beginning to pick something up. For starters, Taylor's hospitality was way over the top. While Steve's story about Tony Sheen had been true, as far as it went, he had omitted to tell Mel about his former boss's underworld connections. As far as he was concerned, what he and Tony had done in the past wasn't relevant. What *was* relevant was what Tony Sheen and Desmond Taylor were cooking up right now.

He decided to see Taylor to try and suss out what his game was, and paced up the incline towards the main house. The sun was high now and Steve, unaccustomed to the humidity and eighty-degree heat, was sweating profusely by the time he got there. He entered reception, grateful for the cool rush of the air-conditioning, and went up to the front desk.

'I'd like to see ... '

He caught sight of his reflection in a huge ornate-framed mirror, tousle-haired, perspiring, dark moons staining his polo shirt under the armpits. Aware that his ensemble didn't show him to best advantage – being well dressed at all times was part of Steve's credence – he stopped himself just in time. Khaki shorts and deck shoes wouldn't hack it. There was no point in presenting himself as a half-baked tourist. He was coming at this all wrong.

It occurred to him that he might be overreacting. Suppose Francis *was* an odd-job man? It would look ridiculous to trot out an unsubstantiated claim that one of Taylor's staff was stalking him. Better to wait and catch him at it, put the bloke on the spot. As for Desmond Taylor, he'd arrange to meet him one evening over drinks or dinner, get Mel to glam up and turn on the charm. Now that would be definitely working from a position of strength.

'Yes, sir?' the desk clerk asked patiently.

'Sorry, forgot what I'd come in for, just for a minute there.' Steve smiled blandly. He glanced around and noticed a display of promotional leaflets. 'I remember now. My wife wanted some info on tours, sightseeing trips, that sort of thing, but I see you've got them all over there. I'll help myself, shall I?'

'No problem.'

'Thanks.' He took a handful and went back out into the glare.

A rustic-style bar by the hotel pool beckoned invitingly and he sat down in the shade and ordered a rum and Coke. He needed to think.

The truth was, the offer of the honeymoon had come to Steve just as he told Mel, but with one important difference. Tony Sheen hadn't exactly got him the trip out of his own, selfless generosity. Desmond Taylor owed him a favour. 'A bloody big favour,' to quote Tony. He hadn't specified what, and Steve had thought it wise not to ask, given Tony's record. That way, he couldn't be a party to anything. It had sounded like an old debt, not blood money. His head had been too full of the wedding to really think it through. Steve cursed himself for not digging deeper. Had he missed the subtext here?

Steve replayed the phone call with Tony in his head, trying to pick up any nuances he might have glossed over. He heard Tony's voice booming down the line, 'I told him, "You scratch my back, I'll scratch yours." Only I scratched 'is first, didn't I? It were a while ago now, I grant you, but a debt's a debt, know what I mean? Course you do.' He'd laughed then, his big man's laugh. Steve had imagined him sitting in a café by the harbour, mobile in hand, his bronzed beer belly quivering.

'Actually, Stevie boy, I did wonder if he'd remember, being as it was some time back, but 'e was nice as pie about it, especially after I put in a good word for you. So we all wins, eh?'

Steve sipped his drink, contemplating Tony's sign-off. Desmond Taylor was giving him what amounted to ten grand's worth of holiday, at least. That favour to Tony must still have strong currency. He drained his glass and got up, suddenly uneasy at having left Mel alone with Francis hanging around. What if Tony was blackmailing Taylor? Tony had gone into the big time, money-laundering – albeit remotely. Far from retiring, his portfolio of wealthy Puerto Banus contacts meant he was busier than ever. Steve still wasn't sure how Taylor had acquired his personal fortune, but it wasn't difficult to guess at a connection. If Tony was holding a gun to his head, taking his mate's new bride hostage would be a useful bargaining chip. After all, they'd only had one day of the holiday; Taylor hadn't forked out that much yet.

Despite the hot sun, Steve started to run.

THREE

There was no sign of Mel back at the villa. Steve raked his hands through his hair, worried now. He went down to the beach and scanned the shoreline. There were plenty of willowy blondes sunning themselves, but no-one that looked quite like Mel. He tried to remember what she'd been wearing – a pink bikini, that was it – and started to walk along the beach, threading his way between slatted loungers and their tanned occupants. He heard a scream and felt his blood run cold, then realized it was just a novice windsurfer falling off a board.

Reaching the end of the sweep of white sand, he turned back, walking closer to the palms hemming the beach. Silently, he berated himself for not having seen this coming. He should never have accepted such a deal on trust – what was he thinking of? He had always prided himself on staying one jump ahead. If anything had happened to Mel ... Steve shuddered. It did not bear thinking about.

'Steve!' He heard someone shout his name and looked around wildly. It sounded like Mel, but where was she?

'Steve! Over here!' Mel emerged from the shallows, Ursula Andress-style, a snorkel mask pushed up on her forehead. He raised a hand in a casual wave and waited for her to come to him, determined not to betray any sign of his fears. She picked her way across the scorching sand, a wide smile on her face.

'It's amazing out there. You really must have a go at snorkelling. The fishes are so colourful. And there's coral further out – this bloke takes you in a boat and you jump over the side and there it is. But you have to be very careful. You're not allowed to touch it.' She stopped to draw breath.

'What bloke?' Steve asked, glancing at the water's edge, where a variety of water sports were in progress.

'That bloke, there.' She turned to point. 'Oh, he's gone.' She shrugged. 'I didn't ask his name. He said he takes the boat out whenever people want. What do you think?'

'Yeah, OK.'

'You don't sound that keen.' Mel put her hands on her hips. 'Lighten up, Steve. Get into the swing of things.' She tweaked the neck of his polo shirt. 'Look at you – the most overdressed man on the beach. You look all hot and stressed out. You've got some serious relaxing to do. Go and change into your trunks. I'll meet you by the beach bar.'

'But – '

She held up a hand. 'Forget the plantation restaurant today. We'll do it another time. And tell Dolly we'll get a snack at the bar so she doesn't need to prepare anything.'

'Mel – '

'Steve. I'm having a ball. Let's just keep it simple, stay around here today. We've got a whole fortnight, remember?' She pecked his cheek. 'Now, what shall I get you? Beer?'

'Make it a rum punch,' Steve said. 'I feel like I could do with one.'

Mellowed out after a lunch of fresh seafood and a bottle of chilled Chardonnay, Mel and Steve sat in companionable silence, watching the breakers hit the shore.

'It's strange, isn't it, just doing nothing,' Mel remarked. 'Bit of a culture shock.' She tipped her head back and inhaled deeply.

'I thought you'd got the hang of it quite well,' Steve teased. 'Comes naturally, doesn't it?'

'Hey! Watch it.'

'Well, you look pretty laidback to me.' He ran his eyes over her svelte body. 'But if you want relaxing further ... '

'Steve! Give me a break, will you?' Mel burst out laughing. 'I haven't got the energy to get up from this table, let alone anything else.' She took his hand. 'Not that I didn't enjoy last night. I did. It was fantastic.' Steve's grin was of Cheshire-cat proportions. 'And what made it so special, for me, was that you started to open up about yourself,' Mel continued. Steve's smile started to fade but Mel was on a roll. 'I enjoyed hearing about your past. It made me realize, you never talk about your family, or your upbringing, or anything like that.' Steve said nothing. She paused, musing. 'I mean, you know all about mine and you've met most of them. Pity Mum couldn't make the wedding, but I'll take you to see her when we get back. And I didn't expect Alex to come all the way from Africa ... '

'Too busy converting sinners,' Steve snorted, happy to move the conversation on.

'Actually, it was my sainted brother who tried to persuade me to get back with you originally, after our first row. I don't suppose you realized that, did you?'

'I never did believe in divine intervention.' She shot him a scathing look. 'Well, it didn't work, did it?' He gazed at her, his eyes a bright, unnerving blue. 'You were the first thing I saw when I came back to Walford. I nearly ran you over, remember? You bitched at me for laddering your tights, so I bought you a new pair. And all the time I was thinking, "I want that girl."' He shook his head ruefully. 'It's taken me two years to get her. Two years, when we could have been together right from the start.' He looked up at Mel again, his eyes shining. 'But I've got her now.' His fingers laced through hers, locking them in a vice-like grip. 'I always get what I want in the end. And this time, I'm not letting her go.'

'I think we both know the reason why it didn't happen the first time,' Mel said, withdrawing her hand with some difficulty. 'Saskia was pouring poison in my ear about you and her – though it wasn't all made up, was it, Steve?' Realizing she was on dangerous ground, Mel continued hastily, 'Anyway, that's water under the bridge now. We're here, on our honeymoon. That's all that counts.'

She leaned forward and kissed him, an explorative, sexy snog intended to distract him from drawing parallels with her own, more recent infidelity. Just to make sure, she added, 'You know, I still can't get over the fact that my name's Owen now. Three name changes in just over a year! Not that I ever felt remotely like Mrs Beale.' She shuddered. 'To think how different my life could've been ... '

'I'd have rescued you,' Steve said, his face serious.

'Yeah? You let me marry the guy with your blessing.'

'Cos I thought that's what you really wanted.' He leaned towards her. 'There's no way I would've sat back and watched that little prick make you unhappy, Mel. I'd have sorted him out.'

'How?' She eyed him, head cocked. 'How would you have sorted him out, Steve? The same way you sorted Dan out – however that was?'

He frowned. 'Sorry, the name means nothing. Less than nothing, actually.'

'Don't muck about, Steve.' She looked at him hard. 'You never did give me a straight answer about how you got rid of him.'

'We had a man-to-man talk. He took my point.'

'You didn't... threaten him?'

'What – "Stay away from Mel or I'll send Billy round with his deadly cocktail shaker"?'

'Be serious, will you?'

'OK. Seriously. That was it. I made his options clear to him and he made the right choice. End of story.'

'Hmn.' Mel's expression was sceptical. When Steve dodged a question, she knew there was more to it than he was letting on. How, exactly, had he presented Dan's 'options' to him? Had he literally held a gun to his head? His words on the plane came back to her: 'If I get a gun and shoot someone, that isn't destiny, that's deliberate.' She felt a shiver run down her spine, despite the heat. Had Steve pulled the trigger? No way. Surely?

'They must have been some pretty stark choices for Dan to disappear off the face of the earth like that,' she remarked, trying to sound casual.

Steve laughed. 'He ain't disappeared. I saw him the day before the wedding. I thought he might've been going to cause trouble for us, but he was asking about Phil. I got the impression he had something on his mind.'

Mel almost breathed a sigh of relief. She was being paranoid about Steve. It must be the Phil thing, making her jumpy. Get a grip, she told herself. Dan was alive. The bad news was, he was back in Walford. 'What did he want?' she asked apprehensively.

'Phil stitched him up. Draw your own conclusions.' He saw her concerned face and realised what she was thinking. 'Don't worry, Mel, he'll be long gone by the time we get back.'

'Yeah. Sorry. I was just being silly.'

He stood up and helped Mel to her feet. Putting his arms around her, he held her close. 'I won't let anyone harm a hair on your head. Ever.'

She returned the squeeze. 'So you're my knight in shining armour. I always dreamed of having one of them when I was a kid.'

'That's right,' he murmured, looking over her shoulder at the sea. He noticed a motor boat coming in with a group of tourists on board. It ran aground in the shallows and they got out, carrying their snorkel masks and flippers. The skipper, who had been steadying the boat for them, dragged it up on to the beach. Steve could have sworn it was Francis.

After the sweltering heat outside, the bedroom was a cool haven. The shutters had been drawn against hot afternoon sun and the tiled floor was pleasantly cold to walk on. Mel flopped down on to the freshly laundered sheets and let the whispering ceiling fan waft air over her skin.

'Aaah ... bliss.' She threw her arms out. 'I'm stopping right here and I'm not moving. Come here.'

'Just a minute.' Steve went to the window and opened one of the shutters. A bar of bright light fell across the bed.

'Hey!' Mel protested, shielding her eyes. 'Don't do that. It'll heat the place up.' She rolled over on to her stomach. 'What's so fascinating out there?'

'Nothing.' He closed the shutters, securing them with a small bolt. 'Just enjoying the view. Which isn't half as good as the one I've got right here.' He joined her on the bed. Mel cuddled up to him, resting her head on his chest. 'Forget it, darlin'. I'm going to have a snooze.'

'In that case ... ' He struggled to get up again.

'No. Stay with me.' Her voice was thick and sleepy. 'It's so nice, just being together like this, all cosy.'

Steve laid back down. 'OK. Though I don't know how you think I'm going to resist temptation.'

'Count sheep or something.'

He sighed. 'Mel. I'm not tired. My brain's too wired.'

'Tell me a story, then,' she said, muffled. 'You got out of talking about your childhood earlier. Tell me about little Stevie Owen.' She raised a tousled head, a smile playing on her lips. 'Was he a *very* naughty boy? I bet you pulled pigtails in the playground.'

'Me? I was a popular kid. Had quite a following. Girls especially. Charmed the pants off 'em.'

'Behind the bike sheds I suppose, in between sneaky fags.'

'No. Never smoked. Or drank.'

'Go on!'

'Didn't need to. What's the point in getting wasted? The other lads did it to impress, but then they didn't have my charm and good looks.' He slid a glance at her from under half-closed eyelids.

She poked him in the ribs. 'Big-head.'

'Common sense. Stay ahead of the pack, don't make yourself vulnerable. Use your intelligence.' He tapped his head. 'That's how I got on.'

'Your parents must have been proud of you.'

'Them? No.'

His sudden curtness surprised her. 'Didn't they take an interest in how you did?'

'You've gotta be joking. My mum and dad?'

'But I thought... I mean, I know you're not close to your mum, but you got on with your dad, didn't you?'

'What gave you that idea?'

'You told me you took flowers to his grave. You don't do that if you don't care about someone.'

Steve looked away. 'He could be a laugh – when he wasn't three sheets to the wind. Which he was, most of the time.'

Mel could feel the pain in his voice. She said, gently, 'I'm sure he loved you, Steve. Sometimes, people just aren't very good at showing it.'

His face hardened. 'The only thing they loved was having a good time. We cramped their style. I don't know why they bothered having us. As far as they were concerned, me and Jacks were in the way. We spent more time with Gran.' He grimaced. 'Closeted in her living room, gagging on the smell of cats, watching black-and-white movies. That was my childhood.'

'But surely your parents – '

'My father,' he said, sitting up so suddenly that she bumped her jaw, 'was a boozer, a gambler and a womanizer. My mother was – and still is – a manipulative, snobbish, uncaring bitch. And that, Melanie, is all you need to know about my childhood.' Two flaming spots stood out on his cheeks. Mel had rarely seen him so agitated.

'I'm sorry. It's obviously very painful. I shouldn't have pried.' She knelt up and put her arms around his neck. 'But how was I to know?' She kissed his forehead. 'I just want to be close to you, that's all.'

'Close to me doesn't mean owning me.' He removed her arms and swung his legs off the bed. 'Why do women always try and do that, eh? Isn't it enough that I love you and want to be with you? Why do you want to get inside my head? I warn you, Mel, don't play that game with me. Cos you won't like what you find.' He stood over her, breathing hard. 'Now I'm gonna go for a walk. You have your nap and I'll see you at teatime. And no more questions. You've taken me for better or worse. Remember?'

Mel threw herself back on the bed, her head in a turmoil. She heard Steve go out and lock the door behind him. A feeling of panic arose in her chest. He'd got the only key! What was he doing, locking her in like a prisoner? There was no need; the resort had excellent security. Was this what it was going to be like, being punished and humiliated every time she stood on his toes? The speed at which Steve could change moods unnerved her almost as much as the coldness of his anger. But isn't it his unpredictability, the whiff of danger, that attracts you? argued a voice at the back of her head. She rolled over, thumping her pillow angrily, and told the voice to shut up.

Steve was going to find Francis. He needed to channel his aggression into something – or someone – and by his reckoning the ubiquitous handyman had it coming. He cut round the back of the house, circumnavigating the entire row of villas – a considerable walk, as they were well spaced out – but found no sign of Francis and his rake. Few people were about: it was 3.15 p.m., and all but the most dedicated sun-worshippers had taken refuge indoors. Steve debated with himself over whether to go up to the big house or try the beach, and decided on the latter. He didn't want to risk running into Desmond Taylor just yet. Best to find out what his man was up to first.

He struck lucky. Francis was asleep in his boat, which he had pulled right up the beach under a large coconut palm. Steve gripped the bow with both hands and rocked it vigorously. Francis woke up with a cry. 'What badness is this?' He struggled to get up, but Steve gave the craft another shake and he lost his footing again.

'Ever heard the saying about not rocking the boat?' Steve panted. He leaned in towards him and fixed Francis with a malevolent stare. 'Well, I don't believe in it.' He gave another mighty heft. Francis clung on to the sides, trying desperately to keep his balance. 'Why you feisty with me, mon? Me give you no bother.'

'Hanging around outside my house? Shadowing me? Harassing my wife? I think that counts as bothering us.'

'No way, mon. She ask about snorkelling and I tell her.'

'So you do know who I'm talking about. You do know who I am. Do you know all the guests staying at this resort? Or have we been getting special attention?' Francis looked shifty. Steve let go of the boat. 'I thought so.'

Francis got out warily, keeping his eyes on Steve. 'The boss ask me to watch you. Him say you the Don.'

'The Don?'

'Like the Godfather filum.' He made an imaginary pistol with his fingers, pretending to pop off a supine sunbather. 'You the man.'

For a split second Steve's lips twitched into what might have been a smile. 'Tell Mr Taylor I'm not a gangster, I'm a businessman, pure and simple. You got that?'

'Yes, sir.'

'And tell him, if he wants to speak to me, all he has to do is ask.'

'Yes, sir.'

'I'll be in the main bar at six o'clock tonight.'

'Yes, sir.'

'And if I see your face anywhere near my house or my wife again, I'll smash it in.'

'Yes, sir.'

'That's what I like,' Steve smiled nastily, 'respect.'

Mel awoke late afternoon with a fuddled head and a feeling of foreboding. Sticky and unrefreshed by her troubled sleep, she padded across the tiled hallway and into the living-room. She saw Steve out by the pool on a lounger and hesitated. Turning into the kitchen, she extracted a bottle of mineral water and a Red Stripe from the huge American-style refrigerator and took them out with her. 'Drink?' she asked casually, sitting down on the lounger next to him.

'Cheers.' He held out his hand.

Neither of them said anything for the next five minutes, and Mel was beginning to boil with indignation – an apology was well overdue – when Steve announced, almost as an afterthought, 'By the way, I booked you a session at the spa. Full body massage, relaxing facial, pedicure – the works.'

She glanced at him. His eyes were hidden behind dark shades. 'Is this your way of apologizing?'

'Apologizing? For what?'

'For yelling at me and then locking me in. Talk about being childish ... '

'Locking you in? Did I?' He shrugged. 'I must have done it without thinking.'

'Yeah? Well, I'm not surprised, you went off in such a strop.'

'I know.' He pushed his sunglasses up and pinched the bridge of his nose. 'Look, I'm sorry about that. I went over the top. It's just that my parents are a sore point. I'd rather not talk about them. It always winds me up.'

'OK,' she said. 'But that's not the only thing, is it? I'm not going to put up with you flying off at me like that. I mean it, Steve.'

He swung his legs off the lounger and leaned towards her, taking her hand. 'You're right. It was unforgivable. The only thing I can say in my defence is ... ' He raised her hand to his lips, kissing it gently, ' ... that you must have made contact with that angry kid inside. The one that wants to lash out at his mother and father for not loving him.' He kissed her hand again, stroking the palm softly with his thumb.

Mel's eyes filled with tears. 'Oh, Steve. I feel so awful. You must have had such a terrible time ... '

'Perhaps it was – cathartic – you bringing it out in the open. And perhaps that was why I turned on you. I felt safe, because I know you love me.'

A tear shone on her eyelash. 'I think this is a watershed for us, Steve.' She blinked, the tear sliding down her cheek. 'Sort of a new beginning. Like I really am starting to understand you.'

He enfolded her in a hug. Mel clung to him tightly. Surreptitiously, he checked his watch. 'I hate to break the moment, Mel, but you've got to be at the spa by half past five. That gives you twenty minutes.'

'Twenty minutes! Why didn't you tell me? I need to have a shower first.' She leapt to her feet.

'But you're going to be covered in oil. What's the point?'

'It's like wearing clean knickers in case you get run over by a bus,' Mel called over her shoulder as she headed for the French windows.

'You what?'

'Forget it. It's a girl thing.'

Having got Mel out of the way for a couple of hours, Steve set about getting himself ready. Showered, shaved and dressed in a lightweight smart-casual suit – no tie, although normally he preferred them: he was aiming for expensive understatement and the Armani was enough – he set off for the Plantation Bar. When he got there, he found the bar almost empty and decided to take his drink outside on the terrace overlooking the resort's manicured golf course. Steve checked his watch: 6.05. He'd give Taylor fifteen minutes, tops. He sat back and supped his beer thoughtfully, watching the distant golfers, who, packing up their buggies and golf bags, were starting to drift home. Apart from the occasional 'thwack' from the fairways it was quiet and Steve, beguiled by the peace, let his mind drift.

He felt no particular pangs of guilt about having fobbed Mel off with some emotional guff about his inner child. Women needed to hear that kind of thing and, if it kept Mel sweet, he'd be happy to oblige. Putting on an act was second nature: he'd been a natural mimic at school – a talent he had used to blisteringly cruel effect against anyone who crossed him – and would have been good at drama, too, if he hadn't considered the subject deeply uncool. Still, the ability was there, and Steve knew how to work an audience, be it one on one, or many. The time he'd cried out to Matt in the courtroom, begging him with tears in his eyes to tell the truth about Saskia, had been a command performance. It had been calculated to manipulate the jury, and it had worked. The fact that Matt was already on his knees after being ripped apart by the prosecution did not deter Steve in the least. Sympathy was a mug's game.

'What's your handicap, then, Mr Owen?' Steve swivelled round to see a tall broad-shouldered man standing behind him in the doorway. He seemed almost to fill the space. Taylor – it was obviously him – nodded towards the green sward below them. 'Fancy your chances? We got some crackin' pros.'

Steve was agreeably surprised to hear an Essex accent. He stood up, smiling affably. 'Not really my game, I'm afraid.'

'Well, there's plenty more to do here.' He extended a meaty hand. 'Desmond Taylor. Pleased to meet you at last.'

They shook, taking each other in.

Taylor was even more casually dressed than Steve in a pair of ordinary chinos, sandals and an open-necked Hawaiian shirt, although his watch and bracelet bespoke of a man who could afford the best. He had a good head of hair for a man of his age – Steve put him in his early fifties – and a youthful look about his big, ruddy face. Taylor signalled to a waiter who was hovering nearby. 'Bring us the ... ' He signalled something and the waiter trotted off. He sat down opposite Steve. 'Nice out here, innit? I always like this time of night.' He winked at Steve. 'Like the calm before the storm.'

'I suppose you go on til quite late up here,' Steve remarked.

'All night and into the morning. Lost count of how many times I've seen the sun come up. Worth it, mind you.' He sucked in his cheeks. 'I've been here over ten years now, and I still can't get over what a beautiful sight sun up is.'

'Bit of a contrast to sunrise over Canvey Island, eh?' Steve grinned.

'Hey-hey.' Taylor pointed at him gleefully. 'I knew it! A kindred spirit. What neck of the woods are you from?'

'Chigwell. We moved there when I was seven. I was born in the East End, where I am now, but I think of myself as an Essex boy.' He shrugged. 'For better or worse.'

'Come on, now. Nothing wrong with that. We may be a little bit fly at times, but I like to think of it as ... ' he paused, frowning, ' ... entrepreneurial spirit. A celebration of entrepreneurial spirit. Living by your wits, that's what all the big fellas do, I'm tellin' ya. Some of the geezers down the Yacht Club ...' He shook his head. 'Have you seen the size of those crates? Amazing. The staterooms!' He slapped his thighs. 'They make *Titanic* look like tat. Even Her Majesty'd be green with envy. I gotta tell yer,' he leaned forward confidentially, 'soon as I went out on one, I was hooked. I said to my wife, "I'm gonna get myself one of these". And I did. Three years ago. You'll have to have a look-see. She's a beaut.' He sat back, beaming.

Steve, who had been thrown a little by Taylor's matey approach, was glad to see the waiter returning with a tray.

'Ah, good lad. That's what we want.' Taylor took a decanter from him. He poured two generous measures and added a splash of iced water. 'Now you don't see this stuff every day.

Once in a blue moon, maybe.' He winked at Steve again. 'Your health, sir.'

'Good health.' Steve took a sip. It was, indeed, an exquisite malt. Mindful that he was being softened up, he decided to cut to the chase. 'You know, Mel and I really appreciate what you've done for us. All those little extra touches. We couldn't have asked for a better honeymoon. And she's in seventh heaven.'

'I reckon that's your department, Steve. Nothing to do with me.' He guffawed loudly.

'Yeah, well...' Steve allowed himself a little smile, 'We can't thank you enough.'

'No problem, mate, no problem. Old Tony gave you a glowing reference. How could I refuse?'

Steve's bland expression remained unchanged by the implication of 'reference'. He took another sip of whisky, savouring the taste. 'Very nice.'

Taylor gave him a look, like he was waiting for something. Steve decided to oblige. Banging the glass down sharply on the table, so hard that the whisky slopped over the sides, he said, 'There's just one little touch I don't appreciate.' He viewed Taylor with clear unwavering eyes. 'And that's the twenty-four-hour surveillance. I've had to have a little talk with your agent about that. No doubt he filled you in.'

'Francis. Yeah, he did.'

'I hope you haven't got the wrong impression of me, Desmond.'

'I don't know what you mean.'

'Only your man seemed to think I was this Mafioso figure. Is that why he's been hanging round the house – looking for sten guns in the suitcases?'

'Nah, nah. Nothing like that.' Taylor stroked his chin, appraising Steve thoughtfully. 'Look, Steve, I can understand you being narked. Francis – well, I told him to keep a low profile, and he obviously ain't done that, so I'll be having words with him meself. He wasn't supposed to spook you and your wife, that was the last thing I wanted.'

'So what did you bloody want? What's this all about?'

'Come on, Steve. You're a man of the world. You don't go taking someone on before you've checked them out, do yer?

I only had Tony's word for what you was like. I wanted to draw me own conclusions.'

'What do you mean, "taking someone on"? This is my honeymoon. Tony gave it us as a wedding present. He said you owed him a favour and this was it: payment in kind.' Steve jabbed his finger at Taylor. 'You and Tony have been in this all along, haven't you? I'll bloody kill him. What's he set me up for?'

Desmond Taylor leaned forward confidentially. 'It's like this, Steve. I got a job for you. And before you say anything, Tony Sheen's got nothing to do with it.'

'I didn't agree to any terms and conditions. You seem to be forgetting that.' Steve narrowed his eyes. 'If you've got a problem, sort it out with Tony. As far as I'm concerned, this is a free holiday.' He got to his feet.

'Hey, hang on a minute. You ain't heard the details, yet.' Taylor waved him back down. Steve continued to stand. 'I ain't expectin' you to do this in return for the holiday. Never mind that it's costing me ten grand. It's still peanuts compared to what I'm prepared to offer you to do this thing for me.'

Slowly, Steve sat down. Taylor grinned. 'That's gotcha interested.'

'How much?'

'Fifty grand.'

'On top of all this?'

Taylor waved a beneficent hand. 'On top of all this.'

'So what's the job?'

Taylor laid his palms on the table, spreading his sausage fingers. He looked down, studying their hairy backs intently, then raised his eyes to Steve. His expression had lost its bluffness and, when he spoke, his voice was harsh. 'I want you to get rid of my wife.'

FOUR

Oiled palms swept up Mel's back either side of her spine, pressing down firmly, but not unpleasantly. Mel felt her breath escape in a gentle sigh and gave in to the rhythm of the movement, inhaling and exhaling synchronously with the masseuse. She allowed the hands to assert themselves, to push and knead her flesh as if that was all she was – flesh, unresisting; flesh that could be stretched and smoothed and rolled and worked until it was as pliable as Plasticine. She seemed to have slipped into a different plane of consciousness: not asleep, but not exactly awake, either; a state of deep relaxation that was like being carried along by a river and drifting wherever the current took her.

She let her mind wander idly and found herself thinking about Steve, smiling at his recollection of their first meeting and the detail about the tights. It hadn't exactly been love at first sight, not for her, but she had been intrigued by the tall, handsome, smartly dressed stranger. Intrigued, and annoyed. He was such a smooth operator, so sure of himself, so convinced she'd go out with him at the click of his fingers. He'd bought her lunch to make up for the car incident – a hamper from Giuseppe's, complete with champagne – a typically over-the-top Steve gesture. Determined not to be swayed by his slick charm, she'd told him his scams wouldn't work on her. The comment had struck deeper than she'd realized: Steve had taken offence and stormed off. Mel, forced to admit to herself that, actually, she really did fancy him, had apologized. They'd made it up and had been taking tentative steps into a relationship when Saskia showed up.

Mad Saskia. Mel still wasn't sure how much was true about what had gone on between Steve and his ex. The woman was a headcase, stalking Steve and sabotaging things between them at every turn. She'd told Mel that her and Steve were back together, that Mel had been nothing more than a sexual stopgap. It had taken a lot of talking on Steve's part before Mel was convinced that he'd slept with Saskia as a one-off. Then just when she'd been prepared to give him a second chance, Saskia had burst in on them in Steve's office, continuing her charade.

Mel, her fragile trust overturned, had walked out in disgust.

How different things might have been, she reflected – not for the first time – if she had stayed! Steve was right, she did tend to fly off the handle. She should have known Saskia was up to her tricks and fronted up to her. If only she'd been less impulsive, less ready to make snap judgements, she might have saved Saskia's life. Not to mention Steve's reputation and all the rest of the fall-out...

'Try to let go. You're very tense here,' the masseuse murmured, kneading the back of her neck with her thumbs.

'Sorry. I got thinking about something.'

'Don't think. Just relax.'

'I'll try.'

'Let's see if some music helps.' She turned on a CD of New Age music. Lulled by the sound of wind chimes, distant bells and Tibetan chants, Mel felt herself transported, until she was floating like a blossom on the foam of the Ganges ...

'Do you mean what I think you mean?' Steve asked, composed. He sat back and folded his arms, eyeing Taylor.

'I want you,' Taylor repeated, 'to get rid of my wife. Permanently.' He returned Steve's stare, unintimidated.

'Wouldn't a lawyer be cheaper?'

'Are you kidding me?' Taylor practically exploded. 'I was nineteen and wet behind the ears when we got married. I'd never heard of pre-nups. And even if I had, I doubt I'd have got one. There wasn't any point. I was just a runner in those days. Delilah made more than me with her modelling and that.'

Steve frowned. How long have you been married?'

'Thirty-four years.'

'Has your wife carried on working?'

'Nah, she gave all that up to look after the kids. Never went back to it. Lost her figure.'

'And you're worth – how much?'

'I think you can see that for yourself.' He shrugged. 'Me accountant's done what he can, but even so. If she gets a top brief, they'll take me to the cleaners.'

'Yeah.' Steve grinned at him. 'Looks like you're stuffed, Desmond.'

'Tell me about it. It's been doing me head in.' Taylor drained his glass and poured himself another, topping Steve's glass up, too. 'I've been over everything. All the financial permutations. How much I was prepared to lose. Which things I could trade her. And then I thought, bugger that, I ain't prepared to give that slack cow half my fortune. She's bleedin' well spent her share already. You should see what she goes through!' He shook his head grimly. 'And the mouth on her! Is she grateful? All she ever does is moan and whinge and carry on ... '

Steve cleared his throat. Taylor was brought back from his rant. 'Sorry, Steve. She don't half get to me. Even thought of getting shot of her meself, at my darkest hour. She's tempted me often enough.' He gave a short laugh. 'Trouble is, I'd be number one suspect. Always go for the nearest and dearest first, don't they?'

'So they say.'

'Yeah, well, truth be told I ain't got the stomach for it. I'd rather it just happened and I didn't have to know about it.' He pointed a finger at Steve. 'And that's where you come in.'

Steve shook his head, smiling to himself. 'I don't know where you got that idea, Desmond.'

'Our mutual friend, of course.' A group of golfers came out through the French windows and on to the terrace. Taylor hailed them in a booming voice. 'Evenin' all. Good game, was it? Who's today's highest scorer, then? I bet it was Chad. Go on, tell me I'm wrong.'

General laughter from the group. 'No, Desmond, you are absolutely correct, as usual. What do you do: spy on us?' The speaker was an American woman with a tanned and wrinkled cleavage.

'Yeah. Hidden cameras at every hole. How else d'you think I know who to bet on?'

The group laughed and applauded. Steve raised an eyebrow. He looked quizzically at Taylor. 'They think you're joking.'

Taylor held his hands up. 'Knowing the form. That's what it's all about. That's how I've made my money.' He jerked his head. 'Let's go for a walk.'

It was almost dark – sunset was early in Jamaica – as Steve and Desmond Taylor descended from the terrace. They skirted the perimeter of the golf course in the gloaming, straining their eyes to see.

'Whoah!' Halting on the lip of a bunker, Taylor turned to

Steve. 'I reckon this is private enough – unless there's someone left down there still trying to dig their way out.' He peered over. 'Nope. All quiet.' He paused, jingling the change in his pockets. 'I'll be honest with you, Steve. When Tony told me about you, I thought all my birthdays had come at once.'

'What did he say?' Steve asked cagily.

'That you'd done your share of duckin' and divin'. That you knew how to handle yourself. That you was respected in, shall we say, certain circles.'

'And?'

Taylor nudged him with his elbow. 'He told me about Saskia, that bird you topped. Neat bit of work, eh?'

When Mel returned from her spa session, she found Steve pacing the villa like a caged tiger.

'Let's go out,' he said. 'How long will it take you to get ready?'

'"Hi, Mel, did you have a good time?"' she asked sarcastically, answering herself, '"Fine, thanks, the massage was fabulous."'

'Sorry, sweetheart. I'm just going a bit stir-crazy.' He dropped a kiss on her forehead. 'There's such a thing as too much peace and quiet. You know me, I'm a night creature.'

'Yeah, Steve Owen, Prince of Darkness.' Her tone was wry. 'Now where did you hide that black cape of yours?'

'You'll be sorry you mocked. After midnight I grow fangs.'

'Ooh, I've always wanted to be ravaged by a vampire.' Mel clutched her throat.

'Later.' He patted her on the bum, propelling her towards the bedroom. 'Go and put on something sexy. I fancy hitting the high spots of Mobay.'

'I'll need a shower first.'

'Another one?'

'I'm all greasy.'

He checked his watch. 'Get a move on, then.'

Mel disappeared into the en suite bathroom, shouting over her shoulder, 'Why are you in such a hurry, anyway? It's not like we've got to be anywhere at a given time. This is Jamaica. Jammin' 'til the break of dawn, and all that.'

He heard the power shower go on. Over the torrent of water, Mel could be heard singing her Bob Marley medley. Steve felt in his pocket and brought out a piece of paper. Picking up the phone by the bed, he dialled a number.

Mobay was as bustling by night as it was by day. A taxi dropped Mel and Steve in Gloucester Avenue, the main strip running parallel with the town's famous Doctor's Cave Beach. Shops selling duty-free goods and crafts were lit up welcomingly, neon signs flickered outside bars blaring reggae and the sidewalks were crowded with sightseers, hustlers, fast-food vendors and street entertainers. Mel and Steve had not gone more than a few paces before they were accosted by a man attempting to sell them identity bracelets, and they were still getting their bearings when a woman shuffled up to Mel and tried to press a carved figurine on her. Steve, exasperated, grabbed Mel's hand and hauled her on, dealing with the hustlers by cutting a swathe straight through them.

'Steve! I can't go this fast. I'm going to break my ankle in a minute,' Mel complained, hobbling on strappy heels.

Steve appeared to take no notice. 'Keep up. We're nearly there.'

Mel stopped in the middle of the pavement, planting her feet. 'You asked me to dress up. I dressed up. Now behave like a gentleman and escort me properly, instead of dragging me along like a dog on a lead.'

A group of Jamaican men standing outside a bar whooped and clapped. Steve glared at them and took her arm. 'I'm sorry, OK? I just don't like being harassed.'

'Just tell them "no". They're not supposed to make a nuisance of themselves. Dolly told me they have resort patrols here, specially to stop aggressive hustling. No, thank you,' she added, as a young girl with a tray of beads fell in step with them, offering to braid her hair.

'No problem.' The girl departed and went up to another couple. Steve muttered something under his breath. 'Hey,' Mel tugged his sleeve. 'It's not like you to get so wound up. Is everything all right?'

He gave her a quick smile. 'Of course it is. I'm on my honeymoon. Everything's perfect.' He pointed to a big international hotel ahead of them. 'I was thinking of this place. It's supposed to have a decent club.'

Mel looked dubious. 'It's a bit samey, isn't it? We've flown halfway round the world, Steve. I don't want to go to some chain, I want a bit of local colour. How about over there?' She indicated a pub on the other side of the road, overlooking the sea. 'Sounds like they've got a live band.'

'It's bursting at the seams. We'll never get a seat.'

'So? I thought you wanted to dance.'

She set off decisively across the road. Steve had no option but to follow her. Music from inside pulsed on to the street through the open door, along with a thick fug of marijuana and sweat. Mel felt the beat throb in her veins, as if her very corpuscles were reverberating with the rhythm. Charged by the bone-melting, hip-swaying bass, she turned a glowing face to Steve. 'I'd say we've just found the hottest night spot in town.'

Still Steve hesitated. 'Look, I'm not sure, Mel. I can't see many tourists in there. It might be a bit dodgy. It reeks of ganja and it'll be crawling with pickpockets.' He glanced back across the road. 'It's best we play safe, go to that hotel. You know what you're in for at those places, and they'll have proper security.'

'What?' Mel was staggered. 'I thought you were the one who liked living dangerously.'

'I can look after myself. It's you I'm worried about.'

'Excuse me? Fending off lecherous drunks is part of my job description. I'm quite capable of handling things myself.'

'Come on, Mel. It's a bit different out here.' He squeezed her hand. 'I just don't want us to end up in a situation. Things can get out of control very easily. We'll ask around back at the resort, see whether they recommend the place or not. If they say it's OK, we'll come back another night.'

Mel set her jaw. 'No.'

'Now you're just being childish.'

'I don't care.' She folded her arms. 'This isn't about where we go, this is about something else. Don't try and deny it.'

A shadow chased across Steve's face. 'I don't know what you're talking about.'

'It's like you've got a secret agenda.'

'Meaning?'

'Don't play games with me, Steve.'

'I'm not.'

Mel's eyes flashed fire. 'I know you. I know how you like to be the one in control. All that ridiculous toing and froing we had last year? That was about you calling the shots. You even booked the registry office before proposing! What were you thinking, that I'd roll over just like that? Doesn't the fact that I didn't give in to your manipulative ways then tell you anything? I'm not going to buckle under just because I've married you, Steve. Putting a ring on my finger's not going to turn me into a meek little wife who'll do your every bidding. I married you – '

'Yes?'

'I married you because I love you.' She paused. Dropping her voice, she continued softly, 'You excite me. You thrill me. You make me feel life's a rollercoaster ride. I like that. But I'm coming along for the ride as a willing passenger. I won't be coerced.'

He took her face in his hands. 'I'll never do that, I promise you.'

'Good.' She smiled again, her anger gone.

'So? Translated, this means you want your own way with everything and if I don't go along with that then I'm some sort of mini Hitler?'

'That's about it, yes.' She pecked his cheek. 'Let's go inside.'

Steve checked his watch discreetly. He seemed to come to a decision. Putting his arm around Mel's shoulders, he said, 'OK. You talked me into it.'

The next few days were spent out in the Jeep, exploring Montego Bay's many and varied attractions. It didn't occur to Mel, who was enjoying doing the tourist spots, that Steve was actively avoiding the Crescent Beach Club and, if he was taciturn at times, she put it down to his irritation at the crowds of garrulous Americans they inevitably found themselves being shepherded along with. They did plantation tours, drank their way round a working rum distillery, rode horses through groves of lofty sugarcane, and, on another occasion, visited the birthplace of Sam Sharpe, leader of the nineteenth-century slave rebellion. Yet another tour, this time of the famous Rose Hall Great House, revealed that it had been owned by one Annie Palmer, a so-called 'white witch' who was rumoured to have despatched several lovers and experimented with voodoo magic.

'Looks like you got off lightly,' Mel whispered in Steve's ear, snorting with barely contained laughter. Steve – who had briefly dated Walford's own Annie Palmer, a diminutive dominatrix who specialized in tongue-lashings rather than whiplashes – pulled a face.

'So that's how I ended up running the health club with Grant Mitchell. Evil cow put a curse on me.' It passed through his mind that Annie, who had also sold him E20 – or the Market Cellar, as it was unimaginatively called in those days – might as well have cursed those premises, too, but he said nothing.

The day trips in the Jeep included a hair-raising drive on winding roads into Jamaica's mountainous interior. The cool fresh air provided welcome relief from the sticky climate of the bay area and they toured through small unspoiled villages where farming, rather than tourism, was the mainstay of the local economy. Unlike the feeding frenzy of higglers and hustlers in Montego Bay, the people were generous and friendly. Mel and Steve lunched on jerk pork and rice and peas in a tinny hillside snack bar and found themselves enjoying the laid-back, good-humoured company of the owner and his wife as much as the simple food.

The contrast with the overblown luxury of the Crescent Beach Club was stark. Looking around her at the obvious poverty, Mel was conscious that the price of a meal in the hotel restaurant could feed a family for a month here. Not that she and Steve were actually having to pay for meals – or indeed anything else – at the resort. Mel had given up trying to keep track of their hospitality 'tab', but she knew from the tariffs it must be astronomical. It made her feel vaguely uneasy, although Steve didn't appear to have a problem with it. Still, the more she realized how much the holiday must be worth, the more a nagging voice at the back of her head continued to ask, So what's the catch?

On the fifth day after his meeting with Desmond Taylor, Steve received an unannounced visitor. He had been taking an early-morning dip in the pool and was knifing through the water in a vigorous crawl when a blurred movement in the garden caught his eye. He swam to the end and stopped, blowing a little. Slicking his wet hair out of his face, he studied a clump of oleander bushes near the fence. They quivered ever so slightly. A magpie flew out of the tree behind them with an indignant, ack-ack-ack scolding cry.

Pulling himself up on the side, Steve swung quietly out of the pool. Casting about, his eyes lit on a smooth, saucer-shaped pebble, which was being used as a decorative edging stone. He picked it up, weighing it in his hand. It was heavy enough to do damage. Without warning, he turned and lobbed it hard into the bushes, evoking a muffled shout of surprise.

'I've got a whole pile of rocks here so whoever you are, you'd better come out before I chuck the rest.' He picked up another stone and took aim. There was a rustle of leaves and a familiar figure crawled out from the bushes, snagging his cap on a twig as he stood up. Steve frowned. 'You again.'

Francis looked nervous. 'Yo, Mr Owen.'

'I told you to leave us alone.'

'Mr Taylor, he sent me.'

'To spy on me again?'

'No, sir. To get an answer.'

Steve dropped the stone from palm to palm, staring at Francis with unflinching eyes. 'Tell Mr Taylor I'm a big fan of married life.'

'Is that all?'

Steve glanced over his shoulder at a slight sound behind him. Mel was stepping out on to the terrace in her bikini. He turned back to Francis with a smirk. 'In my case, yes.'

'What were you chatting to the gardener about?' Mel asked when Francis had gone.

Steve replaced the stone. 'Building rockeries.'

'Let's not go far today,' Mel said, some time later. 'We've been out and about a lot. I fancy doing something round here for a change.'

'Like what?' Steve rolled over on to his side, propping himself up on one elbow.

'I don't know. We haven't really had the chance to check out the facilities, have we?'

'It's all golf,' he said dismissively.

'No, it's not. There's a fantastic pool, with little islands and waterfalls and everything. And there's tennis, a gym – '

'It's too hot for running around.'

'We could just sunbathe and socialize. What's wrong with that?'

Steve caught the note in her voice and flopped on to his back, closing his eyes. 'Nothing, I suppose, if you like hanging out with a load of whinging golf widows. That's what it'll be up there, I promise you.'

'I don't mind if you don't.'

'Well I do mind. I'd rather read my book in peace.'

She prodded him in the ribs. 'Just think of all those wealthy wrinklies lusting after your taut male body.'

'That's what I'm worried about.' He opened one eye, squinting at her. 'Honestly, Mel. I'd rather stay here.'

'OK.' She got off the bed and fetched her beach bag. 'I'll go up there for a swim and see you back here for lunch.'

'Fine.' He blew her a kiss. 'Don't talk to any strange men, will you?'

The Crescent Beach Club's main pool was a limpid blue lagoon in a figure-of-eight shape that had been artfully designed to give a jungle-like ambience. At one end, giant ferns overhung an impressively realistic 'rock' formation, over which waterfalls tumbled into a deep pool. Brave souls could take a slide from the top, and there were lower ledges for the less adventurous to jump in from, or simply stretch out upon. The other, shallower end was tiled on the bottom with colourful mosaics of fishes and marine life. In the narrow middle of the pool, effectively dividing it into two, was an island with a swim-up bar that could also be reached by a pair of rustic footbridges.

Entranced by this fantasy world, Mel indulged herself with child-like enthusiasm, diving under water to examine the mosaics, floating on her back gazing up at the sun-speckled fronds, and then lying on a rocky shelf in the spray of a waterfall. Deciding it was time to sample the ultimate indulgence – a cocktail at the pool bar – she swam over to the row of underwater podiums that functioned as aquatic bar stools.

'Daiquiri, please,' she ordered, taking a seat.

She smiled to herself. This was about as far away from the Vic as you could get. If they could see her now!

'Of all the ginjoints in all the world ... ' said a low voice close to her ear. Mel swivelled round to find a bronzed, middle-aged man grinning at her. He was broad-shouldered and powerfully built, though with a slight paunch, and had a big beaming face. Quite attractive for a man of his age, Mel decided, though he looked a bit of a rogue. She'd heard that chat-up line more times than she cared to remember.

'Desmond Taylor,' he said, proffering a hand. 'And you can only be the gorgeous Melanie Owen. Am I right?'

'Yes, you are. Pleased to meet you at last.'

They shook, Taylor holding on to her hand fractionally longer than was necessary.

'How did you know who I was?' she asked, amused rather than offended. With his smiley eyes and rumpled iron-grey locks, he reminded her of a large friendly dog.

'I make it my business to know everything in my gaff.' He winked at her. 'Looks like you've been having fun this morning.'

'It's an amazing pool, I love it. It's like being a kid again,' she confessed. Her daiquiri arrived and she sipped it with pleasure, feeling the rum warm her insides.

'Tell you what,' he said jovially, 'if I get you a big fishy tail, will you sit on one of them rocks over there, pose for the punters? Cos you'd make a crackin' mermaid.'

She looked him in the eye over the top of her glass. 'Sorry. I don't do topless.'

'I could get you a couple of scallop shells.'

'Dream on,' she laughed, a little reckless with the rum.

'Well, it was worth a try. I shoulda known you'd turn me down, nice girl like you. Steve's a lucky bloke.' He extracted a small cigar from a monogrammed silver box on the bar. Unprompted, the bartender produced a lighter. Taylor glanced at Mel. 'You don't mind?'

'Go ahead.' She frowned slightly. 'Have you met Steve, then? He didn't say anything to me.'

Taylor puffed on the cigar and took it out again, examining it thoughtfully. 'Nah, not really. Not to talk. I know who 'e is. Tall. Black hair. Handsome fella.' He appraised Mel unashamedly. 'You two make a lovely couple, though I say it meself.'

'Thank you.' Mel drank some more of her cocktail, then realized she'd nearly finished it. 'So how come you've kept such a low profile? We've been dying to meet you, to thank you for this holiday. It's fantastic. I can't believe how generous you've been.' She knew she was gushing, but she couldn't seem to help it.

'Thank Tony Sheen, he's the one that fixed it up.' He picked up her glass. 'Here, finish this and I'll get you another.'

'I'm OK, thanks. I'd better go easy, or you'll find me floating face down.'

'I'll just have to give you the kiss of life then, won't I?' He turned to the bartender. 'Another daiquiri, please, George. And I'll have the same again.'

'Don't you take no for an answer?' she asked, flirting a little and enjoying herself.

'No.'

They both laughed. Taylor leaned on the bar, looking out over the pool. 'So where is your old man? Why ain't he here with you, seeing me off?'

'He just fancied taking it easy, that's all.'

'Been overdoing it, have you?' He guffawed loudly. 'Thought I ain't seen you around much.'

'We've been doing touristy stuff, actually. In the Jeep you lent us.'

'I'll believe you. Nice little motor that, ain't it?'

'Mmm.' She launched into her second drink, feeling seductively light-headed.

'Tell you what,' he said, twinkling at her. 'How's about you having lunch with me? Update me on what's happening across the pond. I get a bit homesick every now and again. Hearing about London kinda puts me back on an even keel.'

'Thanks, but I can't. Steve's expecting me back.'

'Come on, Mel. He ain't exactly slaving over a hot stove for you, is he? Anyway, serve him right for leaving you all on your ownsome.' Taylor gesticulated at the poolside barbecue and buffet, from where the delicious smell of roasting meat was wafting across to them. 'Arnold over there has this way with chicken – you ain't tasted anything like it.'

Mel felt her mouth watering. It can't do any harm, she thought. Desmond is our host. It would be rude to refuse after all he's done for us. Besides, Steve needs to know I'm not going to live in his pocket. She looked up at Taylor with a sunny smile. 'OK. But I'm buying.'

He bellowed with laughter, laughing so hard that he had to support himself on the edge of the bar. 'You are priceless, Melanie. Absolutely priceless.'

Mel returned to the villa after a long and boozy lunch to find Steve snoozing in a hammock in the garden. Relieved that he was asleep – she didn't have the strength for a scene – she crept into the house and lay down on the bed. A minute later, the door creaked open and Steve entered, a towel slung over his shoulder.

'Hi. I thought you were having a siesta,' she said drowsily.

He regarded her coolly. 'No.'

'Oh.' Mel tried to gauge his mood, but her brain was too fuddled with alcohol. Steve kicked off his shoes and lay down beside her, not touching. He said nothing for the next ten minutes and, from the regularity of his breathing, Mel assumed he'd gone to sleep. She was just dropping off herself when he suddenly said, 'So where have you been?'

'Mmm?'

'What have you been up to? I expected you back at least two hours ago.'

'Steve.'

'What?'

'There's no need to get het up. I had a swim, and then I had lunch by the pool. That's all.'

'And you didn't think to tell me?'

She rolled over and looked at him. 'Actually, I was hoping you'd come up and find me. Then we could all have had lunch together. They've got a brilliant barbecue there.'

He did not miss the nuance. 'All? Who were you with?'

'Desmond Taylor. He introduced himself when I was in the pool. He insisted I had lunch with him. I didn't think you'd mind.'

Steve was quiet so Mel continued, 'He was really disappointed you weren't there. It sounds as if your friend Tony's given you a big build-up.' She stroked his arm with her finger, drawing the nail lightly down his skin. Still Steve didn't respond. 'Anyway, he's invited us for drinks on board his yacht tomorrow night. You know, that big one anchored in Crescent Bay. It's going to be quite a do.' She studied his stony face. 'Don't overreact, will you?'

He sat up, his expression bland. 'What's the occasion?'

'Birthday party for his wife, I think. Desmond wants you to meet her. He seems to think you've got a lot in common.' Mel laughed. 'Poor cow.'

FIVE

Three water taxis were being kept at full stretch ferrying Taylor's party guests from the jetty at Crescent Beach to his luxury yacht, *My Delilah*. A great deal of forethought had gone into the planning: flaming torches illuminated a boardwalk across the beach so that guests did not dirty their shoes, and the jetty had been bedecked with strings of fairy lights and clouds of heart-shaped red balloons. A band, set up on a platform next to the jetty, was whooping the guests into party mood – a job that required little effort, thanks to the potent rum punch being doled out by a bevy of white-jacketed waiters.

Steve shot a discreet glance at Mel, who was standing on the jetty beside him. Her skin and hair were bathed in golden light by the dying rays of the sun as it sank into the sea and she looked beautiful, glowing. It was good to see her so happy and relaxed, and he reassured himself that he'd made the right decision by not telling her about Desmond Taylor's real agenda. Not only would it spoil the honeymoon – Mel would probably demand they go home, then and there – but it would inevitably bring up the subject of his relationship with Tony Sheen again. And he didn't want that probing.

While Steve hadn't exactly lied to Mel about his past with his old employer, he had only given her the edited version. The truth was, Tony had trafficked a lot of illegal goods through his clubs and Steve had been the one managing operations. It had been booze and cigarettes, mainly, sometimes pirated CDs and videos or rip-off designer gear, but never drugs. Tony had a saying about that: drugs were for specialists and mugs. As Tony's empire expanded, he'd branched out into money-laundering, a much more lucrative scam that he now masterminded from his hideaway in Spain. Steve had been relieved to get out at that point – the going had become too hot, even for him – but Tony had continued to be one of his main contacts in the criminal underworld.

It was Tony who had put him in touch with the bloke he'd got his gun from; the gun he kept in his safe at E20. Steve had bought it to protect himself from his mystery stalker the previous year, and while it hadn't been much use on that occasion – Matt, who had been behind the hate campaign, had found it and removed the bullets – Steve considered he'd got his money's worth since. There was only one language scumbags understood, and a gun kept the message short and to the point. Had Mel known about it (particularly given the circumstances), she would have totally freaked out, but she had no idea he owned a firearm. Only Beppe and Billy knew – they'd had a tacit agreement it might be a useful security measure – and Steve intended to keep it that way. He probably had enough on each of them to buy their silence, if it ever became necessary. If it wasn't he'd invent something.

'Come on, our turn,' Mel said, as a boat chugged up to the jetty.

Steve, snapped out of his reverie, noticed her looking at him with curious eyes. 'Penny for them,' she said lightly.

He grimaced. 'I'd say they're worth fifty grand, at the very least.'

'That's steep, even allowing for inflation. How did you come to that figure?'

'Seems to be the going rate in these circles.'

He said this with a perfectly straight face. Mel glanced round at the well-heeled party guests in their finery – it was a seriously ostentatious affair – and mistook Steve's quip for irony.

'Pound for pound, you're probably right,' she said, laughing.

My Delilah was an impressive motor yacht, even from a distance. Close to, it was positively awe-inspiring. Even the most blasé of the water taxi's passengers stopped talking to admire it.

'*How* big did you say that thing was?' asked a man in a white evening jacket and gold cummerbund.

'One hundred and twenty-two feet,' the skipper replied, continuing, as if he'd been asked this many times before, 'Main deck; sun deck; two salons – one for eatin', one for entertainin' – and two bars also; two dance floors, one inside, one outside, so you can get on down under the stars.' He curved his hands through the air, as if embracing a woman, closing his eyes and faking ecstasy – 'Oh, man.' Everyone laughed.

'As a matter of interest, how many staterooms has it got?' another man enquired casually.

'Six staterooms – one with a hot tub; berths for a crew of six; powder rooms – me don't know how many of them.

She certified for 200 people. And me think Mr Taylor got the full complement tonight,' he added with feeling, prompting another ripple of laughter.

'Sweet of him to name his boat after his wife,' a woman remarked.

'Guilty conscience, more like,' someone else murmured.

'What are you getting at?' The woman, whose fat neck was overloaded with sapphires and diamonds, had turned pink.

'Chocolates, flowers, perfume – you can tell when a man's playing around.' The other woman sounded bitter. 'But then Desmond's always gone OTT.'

'I don't suppose he'd have got where he is today if he hadn't, darling,' her husband retaliated, stung.

'Extremely lucky, if you ask me. On all counts,' Cummerbund said in a stage whisper to Steve.

Mel flashed a questioning look at him. Steve shrugged.

'Course, they can't touch him,' Cummerbund added. 'Impossible to prove. He's got himself well set up here. Pretty much invincible now.'

'No-one's invincible.'

'True, true. We all have our weaknesses – we just don't like to admit it,' Cummerbund chuckled. 'Not that Desmond bothers to keep his under wraps much. Have you seen his latest?'

Steve shook his head.

'Absolutely gorgeous. Legs up to her armpits. And as for her – well, you know,' he finished lamely, catching Mel's face.

'Really?' Steve feigned polite indifference, but his eyes gleamed with interest.

Desmond Taylor was nowhere to be seen, but it was obvious from the air-kissing and rapturous greetings who Delilah was.

'We ought to have brought her a present,' Mel said, suddenly awkward.

'Mel. She won't even know we're here.' Steve accepted two glasses of champagne and pressed one into her hand. 'Let's just enjoy ourselves. Cheers.'

'Cheers.' She took a sip, smacking her lips appreciatively. 'Mmm. It's not often you get to see how the other half lives.' She started to giggle. 'Can you imagine Dad here? He'd be frothing at the mouth.'

'Just as well you didn't inherit his communist principles. I'd have had to have come by myself.'

'No way. Not with all these women about.' She hugged his arm. 'And Dad's not a communist. He's just – '

'A raving leftie.'

'As opposed to a mad monarchist, I suppose.'

Steve blinked. 'Yeah, well ... if they piped my mother aboard to "God Save the Queen" she'd be happy. But there's probably too many nationalities here for her liking.'

'Why is she so obsessed with the royals?'

'Who knows?' He avoided her eyes. 'Used to give her something to aspire to, I suppose. She was always on about us aiming high, bettering ourselves. None of us lived up to her little fantasies so they're her substitute family.' He drained his glass and picked up another one, taking a large gulp. 'You should see her living room. There she is, in this poky little flat in a bloody great tower block, kids running riot outside, and her place is done out like a shrine to the Windsors. Framed photographs everywhere. And you know what? There ain't a picture of me or Jacks anywhere. Or Dad. She cried more when Diana died than she did at his funeral.' He knocked back the rest of the second glass, wiping his mouth with the back of his hand.

'She's the one who's missed out,' Mel said softly. 'Anyway, look at my mum. She went off on holiday rather than come to my wedding. She said she didn't want to be let down all over again.' She stroked his cheek. 'We're a right pair, aren't we?'

Steve put his arms around her and drew her close, his inhibitions loosened by the alcohol. 'We've got each other. That's all we need.'

They kissed, a slow, melting kiss that grew increasingly urgent, enclosing them in a private bubble of intimacy amid the hubbub of the party.

'Now, now. That's too much fun too early. You're making everyone jealous,' a voice boomed.

Mel and Steve sprang apart.

'Desmond!' Mel gave him an enthusiastic kiss on the cheek.

'That's better. Now I don't feel quite so left out.' He beamed at them both.

'This is Steve,' Mel said.

'All right?' Steve's expression was inscrutable.

'Yeah, mate, grand.' Taylor pumped his hand. 'How you doin'?'

'Brilliant party,' Mel gushed. 'And this boat! I can't get over it.'

'Yeah. Beauty, ain't she? I'll give you both the tour later.' He rubbed his hands together. 'Have you met Del?'

'Not yet. She's doing the rounds over there.'

'I'll get her.' He gesticulated furiously in his wife's direction. 'She's dying to meet you. Just don't mention her age. She's a bit sensitive.'

'So why the party?' Steve asked.

'Couldn't let the old girl clock up a half-century without marking it, could I? Anyway, it's no use fighting these things, I told 'er that.'

'And what did she say?' Mel asked, amused.

'I said he could buy me another twenty years by way of a birthday present,' Delilah interrupted him, having come over. 'I've got the plastic surgeon booked for three weeks' time.'

'I can't think why,' Steve said, taking her hand and raising it to his lips. 'Youth ain't everything, is it? There's a lot to be said for ... experience.' He kissed her hand, keeping full eye contact with her.

'Get away with you.' She looked flustered but pleased. Nudging Mel, she said, 'Isn't he a charmer? How do you manage to keep hold of him?'

'She was managing quite well just now. Almost chucked a bucket of water over 'em,' Taylor cut in.

'They're on honeymoon, Dessie. It's what you do. Remember?'

Taylor planted a kiss on her forehead. 'I remember, my darlin'. As if it were yesterday.'

'Bloody liar.' She swatted him away. 'Go and show Steve your fancy radar or something. I'll have a girly chat with Mel.' She tucked Mel's arm under hers. 'Come on, I want you to tell me all about yourself. And that handsome husband of yours.'

Mel looked back at Steve, grinning.

'You do,' Steve joked, pointing at her, 'and you're dead.'

As soon as the two women were out of earshot, Taylor dropped his jovial act. 'This way,' he said, leading Steve across the deck. Two thickset Jamaicans, who looked very much like minders, fell in behind them in a manner that brooked no argument. Steve followed Taylor past the open doors of the main salon, which was thronged with people talking at full volume, along a walkway around the left-hand side of the sun deck and through a door marked 'Private'.

Taylor continued along a narrow, grey-painted corridor, down two flights of steps and on to another landing, which, in contrast, was thickly carpeted and panelled in polished teak. Framed magazine covers, among them *Time*, *The Economist*, *Vanity Fair* and, incongruously, *Hello!*, all featuring Desmond Taylor (looking variously bullish, phlegmatic, brooding and smug), decorated the walls, discreetly illuminated by spots. Steve was given little opportunity to study the cover lines before he was whisked into Taylor's private suite, but his impression was that the man had made his fortune on the stock market.

Once inside the stateroom, Taylor dismissed his two minders.

'Whisky?' he asked casually, crossing to an impressively stocked drinks cabinet.

'I don't mix my drinks.' Steve's voice was curt.

'Come on, Steve. Don't get the hump with me. Have a Scotch.' He poured him one anyway. 'Look, I apologize for the boys. They're a bit keen. Take their duties very seriously, Jimmy and Cyril. Mind you, I'm glad they do. I'm a prominent man. Can't be too careful, you know.' He proffered the glass with a broad smile. 'Nothing personal, eh?'

Steve accepted the drink, his expression neutral. 'If you say so.'

'That's the spirit. Take a pew.' Taylor indicated a curved white sofa. 'Nice to have a bit of peace and quiet, innit? Can't hear meself think up there, let alone have a sensible conversation.'

'Sign of a good party.'

'Yeah, well, if you like chit-chat.' Taylor eyed Steve beadily. 'But you and me's got more important things to discuss. Like where you got to the other night.'

'I don't remember making any arrangements.'

'Cool customer, ain't cha?' Taylor sat back, hands in his lap. 'Let me refresh your memory. You was gonna meet with my man Ricardo and have a butchers at his ... merchandise. Which, I'm told, is the best in Jamaica.'

'Really?' Steve feigned surprise. 'I thought this bloke was just gonna show us the sights.'

Taylor's colour darkened. 'Don't jerk me around, Steve. I speak the same language, remember?'

'I'm not sure you do, Desmond.' Steve's voice was silky. 'Or you wouldn't be trying to get me to do your dirty work.'

'My language, Steve, is money. And so is yours. I find it crosses all communication barriers – if you're prepared to offer enough of it.'

Steve leaned back against the sofa, crossing his long legs in front of him, and sipped his drink. Eventually, he asked, 'Why me and not someone local? You've obviously got contacts.'

'I've thought about it, of course I have.' Taylor looked around shiftily. 'But there's two big problems. First off, word would get out. I tell yer, you can't keep nothing a secret round here. Hire someone to do the business, all they gotta do is smoke a few spliffs, drink a few rums – boom, out it all comes.'

'Police on your doorstep and another set of headlines for your collection.'

Taylor gave a hollow laugh. 'It ain't the police I'm worried about. It's blackmailers. That's big business out here. Any Tom, Dick or Harry could have me by the short and curlies.'

'So what's the second thing?'

'You don't play with Jamaican gangsters. I know a bloke who did, and... ' Taylor faltered. 'Mutilation. Torture. Decapitations. They're brutal.' He shuddered. 'You don't go anywhere near their territory, not if you've got any sense. Besides which – ' He cocked an ear, listening, then relaxed again, ' – none of this is really my bag.'

Steve raised an eyebrow. Taylor caught his disbelieving look.

'That is the truth, Steve. I'm out of my depth here. That bloke Ricardo, he's a mate of Francis's. I've never met the guy. I don't mix with these types. The only killing's I've ever made are strictly financial. Whereas you... ' He spread out his hands.

'And what makes you think I do it professionally?'

'I ain't sayin' that. Just that you got experience. You whacked that woman that was stalking you. And I know you ain't shy about shooters, cos Tony told me. Plus, I've been doin' a bit of research of my own.' He indicated a computer on a desk in the corner. 'Amazing what you can find on the Internet, ain't it?' He winked. 'Your local rag – what is it, the *Walford Gazette*? – seems to have a fair bit to say about you.' He leaned towards Steve.

'I think you're being a bit modest, Steve. Underselling your talents. You're a celebrity. They've even reported your wedding – indirectly. Sounds like it went with a bang.' He winked again.

Steve played it down. 'You know what the British press is like.' Secretly, he was a little surprised, but not over-concerned. The wedding photographer had probably sold a snap to the newsdesk, he told himself. Being found 'not guilty' of murder hadn't stopped the *Gazette* being interested in him, particularly since the ashtray had been found and Matt had been exonerated. Of course, they had to be careful what they said, but they still managed to make sly implications. Steve made a mental note to check the paper on his return. If they'd stepped out of line, he'd have them. 'It's always the same. A bit of notoriety.' He shrugged his shoulders.

'Hey! You're talkin' to the expert here,' Taylor boomed. 'You know how many times I've been misrepresented in the media? How many lawsuits I've had to file? Every time they call me a crook, I sue 'em. It's the only way. Fight low and dirty, cos those bastards sure as hell will.'

'Funny, I gave my best man the same advice.' Steve got up and strolled around the sofa, looking out of the panoramic window behind them at the now dark ocean.

'Did he take it?' asked Taylor, swivelling round.

'Yeah.'

'And it worked?'

'He's still got custody of his son, so yeah.'

'There you go, then.'

Steve dug his hands into his pockets and continued staring out to sea. 'Fighting to keep someone you love's one thing. I can relate to that. Getting revenge on someone who's hurt you, I can relate to that, too. Alot, as it happens. And I never let it go unpunished, believe me.' He thought about Phil and his knuckles whitened. Keeping himself in check, he turned back round to look at Taylor. 'But knocking off your wife just because she don't ring your bell any more, that I can't go along with.'

Taylor got up. 'You drive a hard bargain, Steve.' He walked over to him, clapping him on the shoulder. 'I didn't have you down as being so canny. I think I owe it to you to show my hand.' He crossed the room and knocked on an adjoining door. 'Sophie? Are you decent? Come out here.'

The door opened immediately and a girl came out wearing a crocheted bikini. 'Decent' did not really describe her.

Mel had taken rather a liking to Delilah. She was big, brassy and blowsy, but in a humorous, self-mocking way that suggested she was not the tough cookie she pretended to be. Mel suspected it was an image she'd learned to project over the years; an invulnerable shell to protect herself from the knowing looks and the whispered gossip about her husband's indiscretions.

Delilah's boast that she had been once been a stunner to rival the young Diana Dors – 'Only prettier; she was always so *common*' – had the ring of a woman desperate to convince herself that the seamed skin and overblown figure she now possessed weren't really hers. 'You wait 'til I've seen that plastic surgeon. I'm gonna blow their socks off. This lot won't recognize me.' Her lips curled contemptuously. 'Then I'll really give them something to bitch about.'

She caught herself and gave Mel an unapologetic smile. Mel grinned back. 'You go for it.'

'Make him pay, eh? Through the nose.'

'Through the nose job,' Mel joked. The two women shrieked with laughter.

Delilah wiped her eyes. 'I like you, Mel. Even though you're gorgeous, which usually puts my back up right away. You're straight up.'

'Thanks,' Mel said, feeling guilty at having flirted with Desmond, however mildly. Her loyalties were definitely coming down in the Delilah camp.

'Not only that, you look like a girl who knows how to have fun.' Delilah took her arm. 'Come on.' She grabbed a couple of glasses and passed one to Mel. 'Down the hatch.'

Mel drank, feeling the bubbles surge down her throat, recklessly, luxuriously emboldening.

'Right. Let's show these two-faced tarts a thing or two.' Delilah sashayed up to a good-looking and very muscular young waiter and removed the tray from his hands. 'I'm the birthday girl and it's my party and you, darlin'' – she cupped his face and kissed him on the lips – 'are going to help me celebrate it.' So saying, she took him by the hand and dragged him on to the dance floor.

The grinning waiter, who appeared to take this sudden change of duties in his stride, put an arm around Delilah's waist and pulled her close, gyrating his hips sexily. Bumping and grinding, Delilah, now in full performance mode, tore the gold buttons off his white jacket one by one, tossing them into the air like coins. Then, to a roar of appreciation from the circle of onlookers that had gathered round them, she pulled the jacket off in one skilful movement, and ran her fingers over his smooth gleaming torso.

'Typical Del – making an exhibition of herself again,' a woman's voice behind Mel said.

'You'd think now she's fifty she'd give it a rest and age gracefully,' another woman replied.

Mel turned round and saw two scrawny, pigeon-chested expats wearing strappy dresses and sour expressions.

'If you've got it, flaunt it, that's what I always say,' she sniped, looking them up and down. 'And if you haven't, for God's sake keep covered up. If either of you two proposition a waiter, you might get mistaken for a toast rack.'

'Aah, my angel.' Desmond Taylor extracted himself from the nubile Sophie with reluctance and beamed at Steve. 'Meet the next Mrs Taylor. A major improvement on the current model, as you can see.' He held her at arm's length, gazing at her adoringly. 'Every time I look at this girl I think I've died and gone to heaven. Ain't she something?'

Sophie flicked back her dark tresses and smouldered at Steve with cat-like green eyes that challenged him to say anything different. She was young, lush and long-limbed with the sort of figure that could normally only be produced by airbrushing: a male fantasy made flesh.

'Very nice.' Steve clocked the sultry stare and recognized a fellow sexual predator. Sophie had the self-assurance that only those gifted by the lottery of looks possess; a self-assurance that told him she knew her value in hard cash. In that cool calculating stare, she told him what Desmond Taylor had not. Delilah had to die because that was Sophie's price, because she, Sophie, was worth it. A multimillionaire with only half a fortune was obviously not a deal she was prepared to accept.

'"Very nice"? Are you bleedin' blind?' Taylor pretended outrage. ''Ave you ever met living, breathing perfection, Steve?'

'I'm sure Sophie doesn't need me to tell her how desirable she is.'

Sophie extended a languid arm. 'So you're Steve.'

The upper-class English accent was a shock, as was the greeting. He was momentarily thrown. It could have been Saskia standing there; Saskia, the rich girl gone wild. 'So you're Steve.' Saskia, too, had thrown the greeting down like a challenge – droll, sussing him out. He remembered her attitude, remembered thinking her rude, uppity. He remembered the spark of electricity that had arched between them; remembered wanting her as soon as she opened her pretty, sulky, debutante's mouth.

'You all right, mate?' Taylor peered at him. 'Look like you've seen a ghost.'

'Yeah.' Steve forced a smile. 'The voice. I was reminded of someone, that's all.' He shook Sophie's hand.

'You are a little pale.' Sophie touched his cheek with a fingernail, brazenly intimate. Steve remained impassive. Without looking at Taylor she ordered, 'Get Steve another drink, darling.'

'No, I'm fine. Really.'

'Well, sit down then.'

She was bossing him around, too. Steve remained standing. 'I said, I'm fine.'

'OK.' Sophie shrugged.

Taylor rubbed his hands together. 'All right, then. So. Down to business.' He dismissed Sophie with a pat. 'Just wanted Steve to meet you, my love. As a special friend of mine. Pop and put something on, eh? Francis will take you back.'

Sophie departed with a wiggle of her pert bottom, although her mutinous look – caught by Steve, but not Taylor – suggested such obedience was likely to be short-lived.

Taylor watched her go, waiting to discuss his proposition until the door was safely shut. Steve was amused by the routine. The delicacy was obviously for his benefit and his alone; Sophie had probably set up the whole thing.

'You see my problem?' Taylor appealed to him. 'I gotta new lease of life with that girl, a chance to do it right this time. When something like that comes along, you don't mess around, do yer? You gotta grab your chances with both hands.'

TOP: Steve Owen causes a stir in Walford when he takes over the running of the E20 club and proves himself to be a sharp and ruthless businessman.
BOTTOM: Steve and Beppe di Marco successfully run the E20 together, despite having to keep tabs on a wayward Billy Mitchell.

TOP: Steve has less control over his personal life, though his sister Jackie (pictured with former boyfriend Gianni di Marco) is one of the few people who supports him in times of trouble.
ABOVE: Steve with his mother, after she makes an unwelcome re-appearance into his life.
OPPOSITE: Ex-girlfriend Saskia's crazed obsession with Steve escalates out of control until finally neither he nor Matthew Rose, his resident DJ at the club, are able to calm her and their attempts to restrain her lead to her accidental death.

OPPOSITE: Despite his attempts to avoid prison by blaming Matthew for Saskia's death, Steve finds himself on remand and behind bars.
BOTTOM: Mel stands by him, visiting him in jail…
TOP: …only to witness Matthew's hatred as he attacks Steve in the visitor's room, despite attempts by Mark Fowler to restrain him.

BK7145319
OWEN STEVE

TOP: Both free men, but both tortured by their own guilt and memories. Matthew exacts his revenge on Steve, reducing him to a shadow of his former, confident self. BOTTOM: Clean of drugs and back in control of his life, Steve becomes a force to be reckoned with once more, as he sees off the unpopular Dan from the Square.

TOP: Mel and Lisa are friends, Phil and Steve are rivals in business – and over Mel. But loyalties are threatened when, in a weak moment, Mel succumbs to Phil's advances. BOTTOM: Nonetheless, Steve is determined that nothing will stand in the way of his desire for the glamorous Mel.

TOP: Steve presents Mel with an engagement ring over the bar in the Queen Vic – finally proving that what Steve Owen wants... he gets.
BOTTOM: Mel and Steve – together at last.

Steve shook his head, smiling. 'Nice try, Desmond. But my decision's still the same. I ain't here for business, I'm here strictly for pleasure.' He started to walk towards the door.

'Hang on there a minute.' Taylor went over to his desk. 'I can see I've underestimated you.' He wrote something on a pad of paper, tore the sheet off and folded it over deliberately. 'Every man has his price, Steve. We're both agreed on that. So let's stop muckin' about and talk proper money, eh?' He handed it to him.

Steve unfolded the paper and studied the figure.

'I reckon that's worth five balls and the bonus ball, on a good week,' Taylor said.

Steve continued to examine the sum, as if making invisible calculations on the paper. Eventually, he looked up and met Taylor's eyes. 'I'll think about it.'

'I want an answer now.'

'Then the answer's no.'

Taylor's already high colour went from red to mottled purple. 'And what if I give you twenty-four hours to make up your mind? Will the answer be different?'

'Yeah.' Steve refolded the paper and slipped it into his breast pocket. 'It might be.'

SIX

'You'd better get back to the party. That pretty wife of yours will think you're up to no good.' Desmond Taylor laughed hugely.

'Can I use your bathroom?' Steve ignored the joke.

'Yeah, mate. Through there.'

The sound of a buzzer distracted Taylor and he crossed to the intercom by the door. Cyril, or possibly Jimmy (it was difficult to tell from the identikit shades and suits) seemed to have a problem. After haranguing him for failing to use his initiative, Taylor gave a weary sigh and elected to sort the matter out. 'I'll see ya on deck,' he shouted to Steve, going out and leaving him alone.

Steve had not anticipated this opportunity. It was too good a chance to miss to snoop and he went over to the desk, considering whether to boot up the PC. Predictably, it was password-protected. He cursed under his breath and tried the desk drawers. They were locked. He glanced around the room. If there was a safe, it would be wired to an alarm. There was no point in trying to break through Taylor's security cordon; for all he knew, he could be under video surveillance, anyway.

Giving up, Steve opened the bathroom door – and almost barged straight into Sophie. She had her back to him and was bent over the ornate washstand, doing something with great concentration.

'Haven't you heard of knocking?' She straightened up and regarded his reflection in the mirror, brows knotted belligerently. There was white powder on her beautiful retroussé nose. 'Look what you made me do.'

Sniffing heartily, she rubbed the flecks off with the back of her hand. She did not appear at all fazed about being caught doing a line of coke.

Steve stood close behind her, looking over her shoulder at their faces, side by side in the mirror. Sophie was still wearing her minuscule bikini.

'Take a good look, Steve. Do you still think I'm – what was it? – "very nice"?' Her eyes bored into his. 'You're not very impressed with me, are you, Steve? Perhaps if I did this ... ' She hooked her thumbs under the shoulder straps and started to slide them down.

His hands clamped hold of her slender arms, stopping her. 'I don't think so. I've seen it all before, Sophie.'

'I haven't met a man yet who minded seeing it all again.' She lifted her chin defiantly.

'You think you're it, don't you?' he hissed in her ear. 'You think you can get any man you want eating out of your hands. Well, you're wrong.' He shook her hard. 'As far as I'm concerned, you're just a tart. A tart who'll drop 'em like any other. The only difference is, you're asking a much higher price.'

'That's a bit rich, isn't it, coming from a hired hitman?' Her voice was thick with scorn. 'I know why it is you don't like me, Steve – even if you don't.' She turned to face him, winding her arms around his neck. 'It's because we're two of a kind. We know what we want ... ' she brushed his lips with hers, ' ... and we know how to get it.'

He held her by the shoulders, staring at her with burning eyes. She swayed against him seductively. 'Admit it, Steve. We could be made for each other. See to Desmond after Delilah and we'll run away together.'

'Yeah, and I'll bet you've got the sucker's will made up already.'

'I'm working on it.' Her breath was warm on his cheek. 'Give me an incentive to change my plans, Steve. I guarantee you'll get more than the chicken-feed he's offering you now.'

He took her jaw in one hand, guiding it almost to his mouth. Sophie smiled lazily, then gasped as he tilted her chin up brutally so that the harsh bathroom light shone in her eyes. Pinching her cheeks between hard fingers, he spat, 'I don't buy this crap for one minute. You're just trying to make sure I go through with the hit on Delilah.'

Sophie shook her head, unable to speak.

'No?' Steve said threateningly. 'Funny, but I don't believe you, Sophie. Full marks for initiative and all that, but I'll make up my own mind in my own time.' He let go of her just as suddenly, causing her to lose her balance and stagger against the washstand. Cocaine scattered like snow. 'And another thing,' he added savagely. 'I don't kiss cokeheads. I find it leaves a nasty taste in my mouth.'

'You twisted bastard!' she screamed, scrabbling up the white dust on the floor. 'Get out!'

'With pleasure,' he replied.

Steve rejoined the party to find Mel, egged on by Delilah, attempting to limbo-dance under a bar held by two waiters. The fact that the waiters – both fine, muscular young men – were stripped to their underpants and holding the bar in their teeth did not amuse him. Neither did the fact that Mel was barefoot and had her dress ruched up to the top of her thighs.

'What the hell do you think you're doing?' he snarled, as she shimmied clear of the bar to a round of cheers from her audience.

'Strip limbo,' she said, breathless. 'If I make it under without touching the bar, they have to take something off.' She glanced back at them. 'Get 'em off, boys!'

'Off, off, off!' Delilah shrieked, pissed.

'For Christ's sake.' Steve grabbed hold of her wrist. 'Come on, we're going.'

He hauled her over to the side, where a water taxi was waiting. Mel clambered precariously over the rail and half-fell into the arms of the burly skipper.

'Whoah!' she giggled. 'It's a good job you were there to catch me.'

Steve followed them down the ladder, grim-faced.

'You're out of your tree,' he accused her when they were safely in the boat.

'I was having a good time.'

'You were making a fool of yourself. Is there anyone who didn't get a look at your knickers?'

The skipper, giving a credible impression of being stone deaf, revved the engine, his eyes fixed diplomatically on the shore. Apart from Mel and Steve there were no other passengers and the lightly loaded craft cut easily through the water, bouncing and smacking over the choppier waves. Mel clung on to the gunwale, feeling the spray on her face. She was in no mood to be browbeaten.

'Listen to yourself, Steve! It was just a bit of fun. Everyone joined in.'

'I bet they did. I'm beginning to think your mate Lisa had a point.'

'And what do you mean by that?'

'Calendar shoot ring any bells? Garry Hobbs, wearing nothing but a sprig of holly and a big smile? You were lapping it up.'

Mel was outraged. 'I enjoy male company, Steve. That doesn't make me a man-eater. In my line of work, flirting goes with the territory, you know that.'

'Well, I'm telling you now, rein it in. I'm not having my wife behaving like a slag.'

'Jesus!' She threw up her hands in disgust. 'I can't believe you just said that. You sound like Grant Mitchell.'

He scowled. 'Drop it, Mel.'

'Drop it? You abandon me at the party to go and schmooze Dirty Desmond, you don't come back for hours, and then you get all possessive when you see me enjoying myself. What was I supposed to do? Sit in a corner and not speak to anyone?'

'I'm not saying that.'

She tossed her head, her blonde hair streaming in the wind. 'What, then?'

'Just don't be so free and easy. Men get the wrong idea.'

'Like Phil, you mean?' She hadn't meant to say it, but alcohol had loosened her tongue.

Steve's eyes glittered in the dark. 'Yeah, like Phil.'

'I knew you'd throw that back in my face,' she screamed. 'Is this how it's going to be? If I don't toe the line you'll bring that up every time?'

'You were the one who brought it up, not me.'

'But you were thinking it. You admitted as much.' Suddenly, Mel felt sick to her stomach. She gripped her seat, trying to quell the rising nausea by breathing deeply. 'Is that how you think it happened with him?' she asked slowly. 'Me being "easy"?'

'How else do you explain screwing a fat, bald, red-faced git who happens to be your best friend's bloke? Not to mention your fiancé's enemy.' His voice was heavy with sarcasm. 'Tell me, Mel, because I *really* want to know.'

Mel stared at the bobbing torches on the beach, trying to focus her glazed eyes. It didn't work. 'I think I'm going to be sick,' she said.

'Please, over the side,' the skipper shouted, gesticulating.

Leaning over and looking down into the murky depths, Mel vomited wretchedly.

Several hours later, Mel awoke to find herself lying on the four-poster bed in the villa, fully clothed. The room was pitch black and airless, almost suffocating. It was also strangely quiet. She lay still, trying to get her bearings, waiting for the rocking motion of the bed to cease. It was as if she was still on the boat. Feeling disorientated and a little giddy, she sat up. Her head pounded in protest. Mel groaned, clutching her forehead with her hands. Peering through her fingers, she caught sight of the fluorescent green numbers of Steve's travel alarm. It was 4.30 a.m. Unable to detect his sleeping form in the darkness, she patted the space beside her. He was not there.

Mel felt a wave of panic. Where had he gone? She searched her memory, trying to recall what had happened, what they'd said. She remembered the party, meeting Delilah, getting drunk with her. There were hazy images of the two of them 'dirty dancing' with a couple of black guys, then an outrageous party game which had involved passing different sorts of fruit without the use of hands. She felt herself go hot all over. Had Steve witnessed any of that? Perhaps she had gone a little over the top. The row on the boat was coming back to her, Steve's accusations about her flirting. Her stomach lurched. Oh, God. She'd mentioned Phil.

She swung her legs over the side of the bed and stood up gingerly. Padding to the bathroom, she gulped down a couple of glasses of water and sluiced her face. Her ravaged reflection stared back at her in the mirror, panda rings of mascara under her eyes. She raked her hair back with her fingers, removed the black smears with spit, and pulled off her crumpled dress. Back in the bedroom she slipped into flannel shorts and an old T-shirt, bracing herself for another confrontation. They had to get this thing with Phil sorted out or the marriage wouldn't make it to the end of the honeymoon, let alone survive back in Walford.

Steve was not crashed out on the sofa, as she had expected, nor was he in the guest bedroom. She found him in the garden, sitting on the edge of the swimming pool, a half-empty bottle of rum beside him.

'I'm making tea,' she said quietly. 'Would you like one?'

He did not reply. She retreated to the kitchen and made a pot anyway, bringing it out on a tray with two mugs. Setting the tray on the ground, she sat down beside him and lowered her bare feet into the water. It was deliciously cool. Above them, the stars shone as big and bright as lanterns.

'I never want to forget the way the night sky looks here,' she murmured. 'If there's one memory I want to keep above all else ... ' She reached out and touched the back of his hand tentatively. 'Remember that first night, on the beach, under the stars? It was magic.' Still he did not react. 'And if there's one memory I want to forget above all else, it's us rowing.' She curled her fingers under his palm, clasping his hand in hers. 'Please, Steve. Let's make up. I feel so lonely inside when you cut me out ... '

He turned and looked at her, his face in shadow, unreadable. Mel waited for him to say something – anything – but he remained silent.

'Look, I'm sorry, Steve. All right? I'm sorry if I embarrassed you at the party. I've got a shitty headache and I deserve it. But that's not really the issue, here, is it? There's something going on underneath, and unless we talk about it ... '

'What? You're going to walk out on marriage number two, are you?' he snapped, withdrawing his hand.

'No! But we can't just leave things the way they are. It's just going to fester away getting worse and worse. I know you said you were OK about what happened with Phil, but you're not, are you? And I don't blame you.'

Steve stared out across the pool. His profile, thrown into relief by the glow of the underwater lights, was set: jaw clamped, eyes hooded. A muscle flickered in his cheek. 'What did you expect?' he said harshly, without looking at her. 'A congratulations card?'

Mel balled her hands in her lap, digging her nails hard into her palm, making herself feel the pain. There was no avoiding this. She took a deep breath. 'When you told me you knew, I thought you'd dump me. That's what I expected. In a way, I'm still expecting it.' Her voice faltered. 'It's there, in the background, all the time, eating away at me. And I know it's eating away at you, too, because I know you and I know how much this must hurt.'

'You do, do you?' The sarcasm was thick. He turned back towards her and she was shocked at the fury in his face. 'It's a pity you weren't so concerned about my feelings *before* you jumped into bed with him.' Mel cringed. Steve grabbed her by the shoulders, yanking her close. 'Why Phil, eh?' he hissed. 'I put up with you flaunting yourself with Billy cos I knew it was a wind-up.

Like me and Kat – just a game. There ain't been anyone else for me, Mel. You're all I've wanted, ever since I met you. Then, when we finally get it together, you go and screw Phil bloody Mitchell. You think you know how much you've hurt me?' He shook her hard. 'You've got no idea. No idea.'

Mel's head drooped. 'I'd do anything to turn the clock back, Steve. Anything.'

'Yeah, well, so would I,' he said grimly. 'I'm the one that's got to live with the knowledge that Phil Mitchell's had my wife. He ain't just screwed you, he's screwed me. That, you stupid little girl, is what he was really after. Revenge. And you gave it to him, on a plate.' He forced her head up, making her look at him. 'Do you know how hard it was to stop myself wiping that smirk off his face there and then at our reception? He was loving every moment. All the time, I had to sit there and smile while he lorded it over me, knowing I wouldn't do anything to ruin your day.' He spat the words in her face, spraying her cheeks with spittle. Breathing raggedly, he continued, 'Well, Phil Mitchell seriously underestimated me. He ought to 'ave known I don't go in for public scenes. That ain't my style, Mel, you know that.' His voice dropped to a bare whisper. 'I've got other ways of doing things.'

There was a savagery in his eyes Mel had never seen before. The intensity of it scared her. No-one made a fool of Steve Owen. Her moment of recklessness was going to have to be paid for, somehow. He would see to that. And the price was going to be high. She glanced fleetingly at the water, at the white ripples scribbling crazy, looping patterns across the bottom of the pool. She was a good swimmer, but no match for Steve's strength. He could push her in and hold her under. Serena would find her the next day, floating on the surface. Her death would be easy to explain – a midnight swim, too much to drink, sudden cramps. Mel swallowed, her mouth dry. Steve's eyes were boring into her. She had nothing to barter with, nothing to offer in her defence but her honesty.

'You want to know why I did it with Phil?' she said quietly, struggling to keep her composure. 'Really?'

'Tell me.

'OK. It was Christmas Day. You weren't there. I hadn't even heard from you and I was really, really low after that huge row we'd had. I didn't come on to Phil; he was a shoulder to cry on, that's all. But he – he took advantage of the situation and I, stupidly, did nothing to stop him. I just wanted someone to give me a hug, make it all better.' She sniffed, rubbing tears away with the hem of her T-shirt. Steve's face remained impassive. 'That's the truth, Steve,' she continued. 'I regretted it the second it was over and I've regretted it ever since. It was a mistake, a bad one, a mistake that I made in a moment of weakness, not because I was overcome with feelings for Phil but because I was desperate to be comforted. I never for one second stopped loving you. It's torn me apart knowing that I betrayed Lisa, but it's tortured me even more knowing that I betrayed you.' Tears ran down her cheeks unchecked, falling in fat splodges on the concrete.

'Here.' Steve drew a cotton handkerchief out of his pocket and dabbed at her wet face.

'Sorry,' she gulped. 'I must look a right sight.'

'You look beautiful. As always.' His voice gentle was now.

Mel looked up, surprised at the change in tone. 'What are you going to do?' she asked tentatively.

'What do you mean, "do"?'

'About us.'

'Nothing, silly.' He pulled her against him, brushing his lips against her salty cheek. 'You're not the one I blame. Especially now I know how it happened.' His arms tightened around her. 'Phil took advantage of you.' A note of menace crept back into his voice. Mel shuddered, a post-teary, all-over involuntary quiver. The threat was unmistakable. She was relieved to be off the hook.

'Then why all that business on the boat?' she whispered. 'And just now? You really put the wind up me. I thought…' Mel stopped herself. She didn't dare tell him what she had thought.

'Had to get it out of my system, I suppose. You were right. I needed to know it didn't mean anything to you.'

'Of course it didn't.' She peered up at him through a mess of hair. 'But that still doesn't explain why you were in such a foul mood on Taylor's yacht.'

Steve paused. He was silent for what seemed like an eternity to Mel. A screech owl called out, making her start violently. Eventually, Steve said, 'I took something out on you that I shouldn't have.'

'What?' Mel was unnerved at his sombre tone.

'Come inside,' he said, getting up and pulling her to her feet. 'I can't talk about it out here.'

'He offered you drugs?' Mel did not seem to find Steve's revelation particularly scandalous. 'I suppose I should've thought. There was a lot of it going on at the party. People were smoking ganja like Dot Cotton goes through fags. I didn't, though,' she added demurely, tucking her legs underneath her on the sofa.

'Yeah well, you ain't got my history, have you? Less than a year ago I was out of my head on uppers and downers, and last night our host wants me to do a line of coke with him. It freaked me out totally.' Steve buried his face in his hands, continuing in a muffled voice, 'It all came back, Mel. It's like that point when you've still got a choice, you can go either way. And I knew what would happen if I did.' He looked up at her with haunted eyes. 'It would be the end of everything.'

Mel was stunned by this sudden unravelling of his secret. Steve had kept his drug dependency hidden at the time and, although his behaviour had been erratic, no-one had suspected anything. There had, she remembered, been the incident with Beppe, who had been hospitalized after taking amphetamines from Steve's drawer, thinking they were painkillers. Rosa di Marco had come storming into the Vic, shouting the odds about Steve and drugs, but he had laid the blame on Billy Mitchell. It wasn't until Jackie and Gianni had caught Steve snorting coke off his coffee table that his lie had been exposed. By the following morning it was public knowledge, but Steve had already gone, whisked away by Jackie in the middle of the night.

'Steve, I didn't realize,' Mel faltered. 'I mean, you just went off somewhere and came back three weeks later saying it was all sorted, you were clean. You've never mentioned it again. I had no idea it was still an issue.' She cuddled up to him, stroking his hair.

'It isn't, normally. That's why it got to me so badly, earlier. I was caught out. I didn't think I was still ... '

'Vulnerable?'

He shut his eyes, bowing his head. 'Vulnerable' was not a word in Steve Owen's vocabulary.

'Do you want to talk about it?'

'No.'

She studied him thoughtfully. 'Ever since I've known you,

you've always had to be in control. It's like it defines who you are.'

'There's nothing wrong with that,' he said through gritted teeth. 'Only losers let other people run their life.'

'But the drugs were running your life. That's why you freaked out tonight. It brought it all back, that memory of losing control, of being powerless.'

'Jesus, Mel. Twist the knife again, why don't you?' Steve's eyes were wild, his breathing ragged and harsh.

'I'm not trying to hurt you. I'm trying to understand,' she said, surprised by this mood change.

'Understand? *Understand?*' He spat the word in her face. 'You don't understand. You *can't* understand. It wasn't you there, tied to a chair, begging and pleading for your life. It wasn't you there, watching him pour petrol all over the floor! It wasn't you watching him flick that lighter, grinning like a maniac.'

'You mean – Matt?'

'Yes, of course Matt! And d'you know what he said to me, afterwards? After he'd totally humiliated me and reduced me to – to nothing? That he was "taking the power back".' Steve swallowed fierce, unshed tears. 'And he did.'

'Oh, Steve.' Mel was at a loss as to how to comfort him.

'He took the power back that night, and I lost it. You're right, Mel, I lost control of everything. I couldn't shut my eyes without seeing Matt standing there, telling me he was going to blow up my sister with a booby-trapped lightbulb. He – he had this shoe, and a blouse, with blood on it. He told me they were Claudia's. He said he'd killed her, and framed me. His eyes. They were like the devil's. I believed him. He said we were going to burn in hell together, and I believed him, Mel.'

Steve stooped to pick up the bottle of rum from the floor, but his hand was shaking so much that he knocked it over. Wordlessly, Mel retrieved it and poured the remains into a glass for him, putting it into his hand. The glass clanked against his teeth as he drank.

'That's why I couldn't sleep. That's why I started taking drugs. To blot it all out, make the pictures go away ... '

'How did you get off the drugs?' Mel asked softly.

'Did it myself. Went cold turkey.' He paused. 'Jackie helped. We went down to this place in Cornwall – a big house, owned by these friends of hers. They let us have a cottage in the grounds.

We kept ourselves to ourselves, worked through it.' He looked out of the window at the still-black sky. 'It's probably the hardest thing I've ever had to do in my life.'

'But you did it.'

'Yeah. I did it.'

'How? Most people need clinics, doctors, therapy groups, all that.'

'It's amazing what you can do when you put your mind to it. Plus, we were isolated. I couldn't get my hands on any gear. I had no option but to sweat it out. I gave Jacks the car keys so I couldn't just drive off. She was great.' A faint smile flickered across his face. 'Even though I gave her all kinds of grief.'

'You and Jackie, you're so close. I never had that with Alex. Wish I had,' Mel admitted.

'She's always looked out for me, my big sister. We stuck together. We had to. She was the one who mothered me. And she used to see off my girlfriends when they started coming round. I wasn't so grateful then. That's when we started to drift apart.' Steve's face was relaxed now as he relived the past. 'We went our separate ways, lost contact for a few years. Then we got together again when I came back from France, in 1987. She was with this guy, Doug Bayliss – big Glaswegian chap, owned a string of hotels and nightclubs. He gave me a job, got me started.'

'But I thought Tony Sheen gave you your break.'

Steve frowned. He drained the remainder of his rum pensively. Twisting the empty glass in his hand, he said, 'Doug *owned* the club; Tony ran it. Tony was the one I worked day-to-day with. Doug was more like ... family.'

'Wasn't he Jackie's husband?' Mel asked.

Steve looked startled, as if he'd been caught out. He cleared his throat. 'Yes, he was.'

'So he really was family. That's it, you've reminded me now. She came out with all this stuff about him and you, at the trial, how you were really close,' Mel galloped on. 'Didn't he hang himself in prison? Why did he end up inside? I can't remember that bit.'

Too late, she noticed Steve's clenched jaw and her voice petered out. He got up and left the room without saying anything. Another nerve I shouldn't have pressed, Mel thought, kicking herself for being so insensitive. For a man who had assured her before their wedding there were no skeletons in his closet, Steve's past was an emotional minefield. Still, she consoled herself, at least she knew where the danger zones were. That was breakthrough enough, for now. It was time to give it a rest.

She assumed he'd gone to make coffee, or to get another drink, but when, five minutes later, he had not returned, she got stiffly to her feet and went to look for him. She found him back in the garden, watching the first pink streaks of dawn colouring the fading night sky.

'I feel like we've come a long way, tonight.' She slipped an arm around his waist and rested her head on his shoulder. 'You don't have to tell me anything you don't want to, Steve.' She gave him a squeeze. 'We've got a lifetime to find out about each other.'

'So you still want to stick with me, do you? Knowing all that?'

'Hey.' She pulled him round to face her. 'You've had some bad luck, Steve. And you've had some bad press. But you're not a bad man. I wouldn't have married you if I thought you were. Saskia – she was deranged, I knew that, I was on the receiving end of it as much as you. She attacked you; you tried to stop her. You didn't mean to kill her, it was an accident. And everything else that's happened has happened because of that. Matt – the trial – the drugs ... it all follows on.' She stroked his cheek. 'Anyway, I'd say your luck has just changed. Wouldn't you?'

'Yeah.' He wrapped his arms around her, holding on to her tight.

She sighed contentedly. 'Whatever the future holds, we can get through it. I know we can. So long as we're honest with each other. That's the most important thing.'

He tightened his hold. Mel could not see his face. Burying his lips in her hair, he whispered, 'Yes.'

'No more lies, no more games, no more messing about. We've done enough of that.'

'Yes.'

The sky was growing lighter.

'Come and look at the sea,' Steve said, taking Mel by the hand.

He led her out of the garden, through their little white gate and over the stretch of dewy lawn that separated the row of villas from the palm-fringed beach. They walked on to the sand and stopped, captivated by the sun as it rose over the horizon, casting the first golden rays across the water.

'It's like the beginning of the world,' Mel breathed.

He gave her an amused hug. 'It's the beginning of the day. And we haven't had any sleep yet. Come on. Bed.'

Yawning, they turned and trudged back across the sand. Behind them, *My Delilah* sparkled in the morning sun, standing out clear and unmistakable, like a promise.

SEVEN

As usual, Steve slept lightly. He had not always been such a light sleeper, but the months in prison on remand had changed that. Nowadays, he awoke at the slightest sound, instantly alert. It was a survival technique he'd learned the hard way. This morning, it was the roar of Serena's vacuum cleaner as she went over the tiled hallway; noisy but somehow comforting. In prison, the creak of a bunk or a rustle of bedclothes was all the warning you got. He sat up in bed, strangely discomfited by the still-closed shutters, the cloistered room, when outside it was bright and sunny. Being in a prison cell had also given Steve claustrophobia.

Mel was still sleeping soundly, one leg hooked over the top of the cotton sheet, her mouth puckered and slightly open, like a child. Her eyelashes flickered and she murmured something unintelligible, caught up in a dream. Watching her sleeping, he felt a surge of protectiveness. Whatever he'd promised a few hours earlier, there was a lot of stuff he had no intention of telling Mel – about the past or the present – for her own good. He loved her too much to expose her to that. All the same, he had surprised himself last night. It was amazing how much truth had leaked out with one lie, albeit lubricated by rum. He was going to have to be careful. The border between fact and fiction was becoming fuzzy. If he blabbed like that again, Mel might catch him out. As it was, she very nearly had.

He pulled on a pair of swimming trunks and went into the kitchen. Dolly was there, preparing lunch. She tried to press breakfast on him but Steve couldn't stomach anything. It wasn't just the almighty hangover he was nursing; he was queasily aware that he had a decision to make. Accepting a glass of freshly squeezed tropical fruit juices as a compromise, Steve downed it in one and headed out to the beach. He needed to clear his head.

It was 11 a.m., and the beach was filling up, oiled bodies gleaming on sunloungers as rows of rich holiday-makers basted and burned their flesh. Children shrieked and splashed in the waves and the bay was busy with powerboats. Steve was struck by the normality of the happy seaside scene. Everyone seemed so relaxed, so carefree. Their inertia was seductive. He considered getting a sunbed and stretching out. It was an attractive proposition. He imagined the weight of the heat, voluptuous and heavy, pinioning his limbs and compelling him to lie there, immobile and unresisting. If he shut his eyes and surrendered himself to the sun, would this decision go away?

'Look!' a small boy cried excitedly, pelting past Steve with his little sister in tow. Steve looked to where they were pointing. A cloud of red, heart-shaped helium balloons, trailing foil ribbons, was rising from the jetty. They drifted and separated, spreading out across the bay as the gentle breeze caught them and carried them upwards.

Steve watched, straining his eyes to see, as they soared higher and higher, until all he could make out was a pattern of red specks, vivid against the blue, blue Caribbean sky. It made him feel felt oddly exhilarated, as if his problem had flown away with the balloons. All of a sudden, his lassitude had gone.

Smiling to himself, he strode across the powdery white sand and plunged into the sea. The water was warm and calm, not so much bracing as embracing, folding him to the soft swell of its bosom with light lapping waves. He struck out a little distance from the crowded water's edge, enjoying the solitude of the deeper water. Flipping over on to his back he relaxed, letting his body go limp and his legs float up to the surface. Spread-eagled like a starfish, he allowed the ocean to cushion and carry him. It was restorative being so weightless, so insubstantial. The water in his ears deadened his hearing, tuning out the world above and around him, and internalizing all noise to a series of sloshes and glugs. He was utterly alone with himself.

Steve was drinking an ice-cold beer in the shade of the beach bar when Desmond Taylor caught up with him. He had noticed the motor boat come in, but had thought nothing of it at the time – boats went to and from the beach's small landing stage constantly, many of them hired by the resort's guests for exploring the coastline. He was taken aback at seeing Taylor again so soon. The twenty-four hour deadline was not nearly up. He was even more surprised to see that Desmond was accompanied by Delilah.

'Steve! We meet again!' Taylor clapped him on the back. 'How are you this morning? Suffering?'

'I'm working on a cure.' He saluted Taylor with his beer.

'Excellent idea, mate. I could do with one of those myself. Del? Hair of the dog?'

Delilah, who was hiding behind a large straw hat and dark glasses, shook her head. 'I'll have a Coke.'

'She's feelin' a bit fragile this morning. Ain'tcha?' he boomed.

Delilah winced. Taylor seemed not to notice. 'Mind if we join you?' He pulled up a chair.

'Be my guest,' Steve answered, not given the option.

'Ha, ha,' Taylor laughed. He signalled to a waiter and ordered drinks, insisting on getting Steve another beer. 'Where's young Melanie, then? Sleeping it off?'

Steve nodded. 'Is she OK?' Delilah asked.

'She'll live.'

'I feel responsible.' Delilah rummaged in her shoulder bag and produced a small brown bottle. 'Give her this. Tell her to put ten drops on her tongue. It works wonders.'

'She don't go anywhere without that stuff.' Taylor nudged his wife. 'Do you?'

'For God's sake. You make me sound like a bloody alkie.'

Taylor grinned, making a secret drinking gesture to Steve.

Delilah ignored him. 'Give Mel my love. I think I led her astray a bit last night. I hope you weren't too hard on her.'

'So it's you Steve should be punishing, is it? Smack bottom for Del.' Taylor seemed to find this uproariously funny.

Delilah shot him a savage look. 'If a woman can't go a bit mad on her fiftieth birthday ... It's all downhill from here; I might as well go out in style.'

'Yeah, you're right, love.' Taylor was suddenly sober. 'You deserved to push the boat out.' He drank his beer, staring out to sea.

'It was a great party. We really enjoyed it,' Steve said to Delilah. 'Good crowd, too. You've obviously made a lot of friends here.'

She wrinkled her nose. 'A lot of them are hangers-on. That's what it tends to be like. They're all over you at the time, "Oh darling, you must come and visit us in Antibes." Or wherever. Then they bugger off. And do we get an invite? Do we heck. Too common,' she whispered, leaning towards him. 'Me and him.' She nodded at Desmond, who seemed to have gone into a trance over his beer. 'They like our money, love our resort, but all we're fit for is dinner-party gossip. I know what they talk about. I know *exactly* what they say. *Bitches!*' She slammed her palm down on the table, making the beer bottles jump. 'That's why I like Mel. There's no side to her. I noticed that straight off.'

'I know. She's totally genuine. That's one of the things I love about her.' He meant it, Steve realized. He'd never analysed why he felt about Mel the way he did – she was gorgeous, there was a physical attraction, obviously, but it went much deeper than that. Once again, his subconscious seemed to be speaking out of turn. It was disconcerting.

'You're lucky. I wish ... ' Delilah hesitated. 'Sometimes I wish we hadn't got all this. Things would be so much simpler. And you'd know who your friends really were.'

'Don't be so bloody daft, woman,' Desmond interrupted. 'You wouldn't last two minutes without your gold Amex card and a chauffeur-driven Merc.'

'That's two minutes longer than you'd last, then,' she hissed. 'Do you think any of those tarts would come near you if you weren't loaded?'

Taylor stood up, his face ruddier than usual. 'I'll ignore that, on the grounds you ain't feelin' yourself. I got work to do, up the house. What are you up to today, my son?' He gave Steve a significant look.

Steve shrugged. 'Taking it easy, I should think.'

'Ahhh ... it's all right for some. Here you are, soakin' up the rays, and I've gotta get down to business.'

'He is on his honeymoon,' Delilah reminded him.

'Yeah, yeah, I know. He deserves his leisure time, does Steve.' Taylor winked. 'Anyhow, I ain't got cause for complaint. Beautiful place like this to commute to from me yacht. Well, I'll see you later, then.' He made as if to go, then turned round again. 'You know, Steve, if you ain't got nothin' better to do, and Mel's still got her head down, why don't you get Del to take you out in the boat? Blow the old cobwebs away.'

Steve regarded him suspiciously. He had been waiting for some sort of cue. Taylor's face was open, friendly. What was he playing at?

'Have you seen the coastline around here? Stunning. It's stunning, ain't it, Del? Especially if you head eastwards, out beyond

Falmouth. Discovery Bay, now that's a good one. That's where Columbus first discovered Jamaica. Really wild, amazing cliffs.'

'Mmm. Runaway Bay, that's pretty, too,' Delilah agreed. She brightened. 'There's a fantastic beach bar there. They serve grilled seafood that's so fresh it's straight out of the net.'

'I don't know ... I wouldn't want to put you out. You must have got plans, yourself,' Steve said cagily.

She yawned. 'Not really. I was going to have a spa session, get rid of some of the toxins, that's all.'

'There you are then,' Taylor said. 'A dose of sea air in your lungs will do the job just as well and much cheaper – since you're after the simple life.'

'Just can't resist the sarky comment, can you?' she retorted. She turned to Steve. 'I'll do it for you, Steve, if you want. Not because *he's* suggested it. Because I like you. I quite fancy a change of scenery, actually. Anything's got to be better than the view I have to put up with, day in and day out.'

'Watch it, Steve. I think she likes you,' Taylor jested, impervious.

Steve flicked a glance at him. He still wasn't sure what Taylor intended. He decided to call his bluff.

'I'll go and see if Mel's surfaced, shall I? Be nice to make a day of it.' He smiled at Delilah, turning on the charm. 'Especially as you two get on so well.'

'Fine by me. I'm too fagged to move. I'll have a coffee, wait for you both here.'

Taylor did not try to counter this suggestion. Instead, he said, 'Good. That's sorted, then,' and stooped to peck Delilah on the cheek.

'What's that for? Guilty conscience?' she snapped.

He sighed. 'Just can't win, can I? Come on, Steve. I'll walk with you.' Laying a heavy arm across his shoulders, he steered him across the beach.

'Let's take the scenic route.' Taylor took a left, away from the row of villas, following a path through dense shrubbery and overhanging vines. Steve, brushing trailing leaves off his face, walked behind, breathing in the hot, earthy, crushed-herb smell of the vegetation. Lurid blossoms, flaunting their vulgarly exposed stamens, perfumed the humid air sickly-sweet. A myriad buzzing insects darted and hovered in the shafts of light falling through the greenery. Steve trod carefully, concerned about snakes. Runnels of sweat slid down his spine. It occurred to him that Taylor might have set up some sort of rendezvous – perhaps with the illegal firearms dealer he was meant to have met before – and he felt uneasy. This wasn't the way he wanted to do things.

The path wound quite steeply uphill and emerged suddenly on to the smooth green grass of the golf course, which extended all the way to the edge of the cliff.

'See where we are now?' Taylor pointed further up the hill, to where the main house was situated.

'Yeah.' Steve tried to control his panting. He did not want to appear out of breath. He needn't have worried. Taylor, was perspiring profusely, his chest heaving with the effort of the climb.

'Bit of a hike, but it's worth it. Great view, eh?' Taylor indicated the sparkling Caribbean below them. 'I like to come up here and cogitate sometimes. Helps get things in perspective.'

Taylor led the way to a bench, which had been set on a levelled out area overlooking the sea. He took a packet of cigarettes out of his shirt pocket and offered one to Steve, who refused. 'Sensible chap.' He patted his other pocket, feeling for his lighter. 'What's the point of having a fortune if you're gonna throw your life away smoking this stuff?' He lit up, inhaling deeply and exhaling slowly with obvious satisfaction. 'Crazy, innit? But then you gotta figure out what it is that makes your life worth living in the first place. No use living to a hundred if you're unhappy, is there?'

'Live now, pay later?'

'Exactly.'

'What if you have to pay now?'

'What are you getting at?' Taylor eyed him suspiciously.

'Nothing. My mother's got heart disease from smoking. She's probably only ten years or so older than you.'

'Then I hope she had a good time getting it,' he said callously.

'My mother's never had a good time doing anything. Apart from making her kids suffer.' Steve's voice was bitter.

Taylor registered the tone, the bleak expression. 'Some folk are just like that, Steve. They have a downer on everyone. Personally, I think they should be put out of their misery. I mean, what do they do, apart from sitting around, criticizing, making people unhappy?' He shot him a calculating glance. 'Del, for instance. There's no pleasing her. She's a right miserable cow. Sounds like your old lady.'

Steve did not comment.

Taylor blew an impressive smoke ring, watching it drift and dissolve. Casually, he said, 'What did you make of Sophie, then? Really?'

'She's a babe. You're a lucky man, Desmond.'

'I'm a lucky man, but my luck's running out, Steve. As you so correctly point out, Sophie is a babe. And a babe like that ain't gonna hang around for ever. In fact, if I don't get somethin' sorted about Del within the next week, she's walkin'. So she says. Gave me an ultimatum last night, after you'd gone.' He turned to face him. 'She seemed ... upset. Wouldn't say why. I dunno – she can be a temperamental little thing at times. Said she wanted to know where she stood. Well, I know what *that* means.' He glanced behind them, making sure there were no golfers within earshot. 'Sophie is my life. She is what makes my existence worthwhile. I know it won't last – she might stick with me five years, maybe ten, if I keep meself fit. But I'll take that deal. I don't care what happens after that. That's what I want. And that's what I'm prepared to pay you for.'

Steve smiled. 'Come on, Desmond. It's a small price for you, financially. What about Delilah? What about the price she has to pay?'

Taylor threw down his cigarette butt, got up and ground it into the grass with his heel. 'That ain't your concern, Steve.' He shoved his hands in his pockets, staring out to sea. 'Look, you're a decent bloke. You've got qualms, and that's as it should be. I can see you don't go into anything lightly, and I respect that.'

Steve could not tell whether Taylor was taking the piss or just trying to butter him up. He got to his feet and stood beside him. 'We said twenty-four hours, Desmond. I'll tell you tonight.'

Taylor seemed not to hear him. 'I ain't slept a wink thinking about this. I can't let Sophie go. I want to ring her tonight, tell her the way's clear.' His eyes were haggard, almost pleading. 'That figure's still on the table. Plus I'll throw in a fortnight's free holiday here, every year for the next ten years.'

Steve pursed his lips. Taylor looked away again.

'It needn't be a big, messy job, Steve. Accidents happen.

Delilah – she ain't much of a swimmer. Never goes out of her depth in the water. And the currents off the north coast are strong this time of year. There's a headland after Rio Bueno harbour, before you dip down to Discovery Bay. That's where they're the worst. And you ain't overlooked by hotels or nothing, so it'd be real hard to get help there.'

Steve studied the azure ocean. So that's what the gig with Delilah and the boat was. He stood there for a long time without speaking. Finally, he said, 'No more holidays. I want the cash value. That's another £100,000 by my reckoning. We won't be coming here again.'

Mel was still asleep when Steve returned to the villa. He dressed in a short-sleeved shirt, shorts and deck shoes and grabbed a baseball cap and shades for good measure. Thinking his mission through, he stuffed a change of clothing in a bag, along with a different hat. It would help not to be recognized on his return. He moved swiftly and quietly, doing his best not to disturb Mel. If she awoke, he'd have to find some excuse to reschedule the boat trip, plus he'd have to arrange to get her out of the way. It was complicated enough as it was. Delilah might have got bored waiting for him and gone off to do her own thing. There was one other compelling reason for not delaying. His blood was up. If he was going to do this thing, it had to be now.

An hour ago, floating in the sea, he'd been undecided. The money was an inducement, a very tempting inducement, but something had been holding him back. He was capable of taking extreme measures, he knew that. He had been to the brink, more than once. He had been there by accident, and had been there by design. But each time he had been there, the motivation had been personal. To a man wavering on the edge, to a man who very much wanted to take the money, Taylor had just made it personal. Never mind the skewed logic, the emotional manipulation; Steve was clever enough to see that for what it was. He even admired Taylor's crude tactics. They were an admission – 'I know that you know that I know' – which acknowledged something deeper: a primitive nerve that bypassed reason and went straight to the heart.

Mel stirred and sighed, stretching out her limbs. Steve froze. She turned over on to her face with a slight groan, flinging one arm out to the side and knocking a glass of water on the bedside table. The glass rocked, sloshing water. Steve held his breath. It did not fall. He allowed himself to breathe again. Waiting until her own breathing had settled back into a regular pattern, he crept stealthily out of the room. There was an antique writing desk in the living-room, equipped with stationary. He took a pad of paper and scribbled a hasty note:

Dear Mel, Gone to the beach – might try snorkelling, as you raved about it so much. Back teatime, love, Steve.
PS. Put your feet up and chill out this afternoon – we'll go somewhere special for dinner. XXX.

He left the note in the kitchen where she would see it, told Serena not to make any more noise and set off to find Delilah. Fortunately, she was still at the bar.

'I'd almost given up on you,' Delilah greeted him sharply. 'Where's Mel?'

'Still in bed. Sorry I was so long – I was hoping she'd join us. I got her sat up and gave her a cup of tea but she laid back down again when my back was turned. Next thing I knew – ' he clicked his fingers, ' – out like a light again. Short of frog-marching her into the shower there was nothing I could do.'

'I'd've thought she was built of sterner stuff.' Delilah got to her feet, swaying slightly. Steve noticed an empty wine bottle on the table. She saw him looking. 'Don't worry about that. I'll need another before I'm even operating at peak capacity.'

'In that case, we'll sink a couple of bottles of chilled Chablis in Runaway Bay over a big lobster salad and you can let me sail us home again.' He smiled a slow sexy smile. 'But you'd better give me a lesson on the outward trip, just to let me get the hang of it.'

'With pleasure.' Delilah tucked her arm into his. 'It's nice to be made a fuss of. I think the day's looking up.' Squeezing his arm, she continued, 'Actually, I'm rather glad Mel can't make it. Means I've got you all to myself.' She straightened her hat and squared her shoulders, turning a stern face to him. 'But there's one thing I'll warn you now.'

'What's that?' Steve asked warily, his heart speeding up ever so slightly.

'You won't get Chablis in Runaway Bay.' She headed for the

bar. 'We'll take some with us. There's an icebox on board.'

He watched as she ordered four bottles of wine and two six-packs and instructed a waiter to carry them to the boat. This was going to be easier than he thought. If she drank half that amount she'd probably trip overboard by herself. All it would take would be one little push and Mrs Delilah Taylor would drown in a tragic, but inevitable, accident.

EIGHT

The boat, a sixteen-foot outboard skiff named *Delilah Too*, was tied up at the jetty.

'This is just the runaround. We should take the launch really, but she's having some work done on the hull,' Delilah said, getting in.

'How many boats have you got?' asked Steve.

'Three. No, four. Des keeps a sailing dinghy down at the Yacht Club. This one's seaworthy, though, so long as we stay near the coast.'

'Glad to hear it,' Steve said, clambering in beside her. 'My days with the Sea Scouts are long gone.'

The waiter who had carried the booze consignment untied the rope and threw it to Steve who looked at it, nonplussed.

'Coil it up and put it over there,' Delilah said, indicating a hook. She started the outboard engine, shouting over the top, 'Your days with the Sea Scouts were non-existent.'

He smiled, saying nothing. The boat took off from the jetty with a flourish, cutting a wide wake that made the other craft moored there bob up and down. They headed out to sea with the sun on their faces and the breeze rippling their clothes, Delilah jamming her straw hat down firmly on her head.

'This is the life!' she yelled, a broad grin on her face.

It made a change to see her looking happy. From what he'd seen of her so far, Delilah's normal expression was piqued. Steve looked away again. He didn't want to relate to this woman, or think about her, or attempt to understand her. He just wanted to get the job over and done with.

'How far is it to Runaway Bay?' he asked, thinking of the instructions Desmond Taylor had given him.

'About fifty kilometres. At this speed we should be there in an hour or so.'

'Gotta map? I'd like to see where we're going.'

'Here you are.' She passed him a dog-eared copy of *Jamaica Coastal Charts*. 'We're heading towards Falmouth.'

'I see it. Right.' He made a few swift calculations. It might be easier to carry this out after lunch, on the way back. She'd be far more sozzled by then. At the moment, she was looking pretty chipper. 'Drink?' He opened the cooler.

'Thought you'd never ask.'

He poured her a large glass. 'So, can I have a go, then?'

She changed places, giving him the tiller. 'Just remember to pull it the opposite way to the direction you want to go in. That's all there is to it.'

For a while they continued without talking, both of them caught up in their own worlds. Delilah seemed content to sit drinking wine, her face tipped up to the sun, while Steve, beer in hand, guided the little boat in the shadow of the tall white cliffs.

'Having fun?' she asked lazily, watching him hail another boat with a casual wave.

'Makes a change.'

'Bit different from dodging traffic in London.'

'You're not kidding.'

'Mel told me you run a nightclub in the East End.'

'That's right.'

'Popular?'

'It doesn't do too badly. Built up a solid reputation. Actually, I'm thinking of expanding. Maybe buy a couple more in the area.' He said it without a flicker.

She poured another glass of wine. 'You must like the lifestyle then. I hope Mel does, for her sake.'

'Yeah, well, early days. We ain't really discussed it yet.'

'I used to find it exhilarating, but it isn't everyone's cup of tea. You've really got to be a night creature.'

'You used to work in a nightclub?' Steve was surprised. 'Desmond said you'd been a model.'

She laughed heartily. 'He's got a selective memory. I was a model, in the loose sense of the term. I was a pretty girl. I made good use of my looks.' She preened her ash-blonde hair.

'You were an escort?'

'Escort, hostess, bunny girl, call 'em what you will. Ended up as a greeter in a swish West End joint. Very glam. Absolutely adored it.'

'I used to have a West End club. Off Regent Street.'

'Really? There you are, then: we're kindred spirits. I thought there was something, when I met you.'

'The old secret handshake, eh? Never fails.'

'Is that what you call it? And I thought you were just being charming.'

She was flirting with him. Steve found he didn't mind. Delilah wasn't the dragon that Taylor had made her out to be. She cocked her head on one side, appraising him.

'Y-es. I can see you running a club. You've got the charm, the looks, the nous. You would know how to play it.' She leaned forward, revealing – deliberately, Steve thought – a glimpse of ample cleavage. 'And,' she said insinuatingly, 'I bet you're as hard as nails under that sleek outer skin, aren't you?'

He smiled, shaking his head. 'You can read me like a book, Delilah.'

'I've had plenty of practice.' She drained the last of the bottle into her glass. 'I used to go out with a bloke like you, before I met Des. Couldn't make him commit. He was a right slippery customer. I reckon Mel's lucky to have nailed you down.'

She passed Steve another beer can. He opened it thoughtfully. Talking about himself was a novelty; normally he avoided it like the plague. As far as he was concerned, divulging personal details merely gave other people power over you. This situation, though, was rather different. He wouldn't be meeting Delilah again.

'I think I'm the one that's lucky to have got Mel.' He shrugged. 'I admit it, I used to play the field. Nightclubs ... well, you know how it is.'

'Easy come, easy go.'

'Yeah.'

'And you never found anyone special?'

He hesitated.

'One.'

'So what happened?'

'She was ... extreme. Behaved as if life was a non-stop party. I liked that, at first. We had a ball. Then, when we settled down, I found out she really was crazy.'

'So you chucked her.'

'Not at first. I tried to help her get straight. But she was taking drugs and drinking and it got out of control. I'd come home and she'd be hysterical, a total wreck. I was struggling to keep the club afloat, and I just couldn't deal with it. Then she started sleeping around and that was that.'

'Have you seen her since?'

Steve crumpled up his beer can and hurled it into the sea. 'She's dead.'

'Oh.' Delilah was taken aback. 'Was it – the drugs?' She sighed. 'So destructive. The poor girl.'

'Don't waste your breath,' he said brutally. 'She brought it on herself.'

When Mel found Steve's note she felt inexplicably let down. She reasoned to herself that she was the one who'd made an issue about doing her own thing, but even so she felt hurt. After the soul-baring of the night and seeing in the dawn together, the two of them had never been so close. It was as if a whole new chapter of their lives was opening up. They had gone back to the villa and made love, and the sex had had a different quality, tender, almost tentative, as if they were rediscovering each other's bodies as well as their minds. The last thing Mel remembered was falling asleep in Steve's arms. Then, when she awoke, he was gone. All things considered, she felt she had a right to be a bit miffed.

It was a typical *Men Are From Mars, Women Are From Venus* scenario, she thought, as she got into the shower. Once Steve allowed her into his heart, he had to rebound again, reassert his masculinity or whatever it was men did. Pathetic, really. She turned on the water full volume, dousing her hair and letting the needle-sharp spray pummel her circulation.

I bet he isn't like that with Jackie, she thought, with a stab of jealousy. The bond between Steve and his sister was a formidable one. It was Jackie he'd spent Christmas with, leaving her, his fiancée, to the mercy of Phil Mitchell. It was Jackie who'd helped him get off drugs. It was Jackie's testimony that had got Steve off the charges of killing Saskia, if you listened to most people in the Square. And it was Jackie who had worked to reintegrate him afterwards, inviting him on the stags and hens trip when most people weren't even speaking to him.

Mel lathered shower gel over her skin, remembering the trip to Amsterdam. She'd been about to marry Ian, but it was Steve she'd wanted, in her heart of hearts. She'd got drunk and asked him to kiss her, but he had refused. Had it been chivalry, as she'd always supposed? Or was he playing games, even then? Their courtship, such as it was, had been tactical right from the start.

Attacks and counter-attacks, trading pieces, one making a move, the other blocking it, like a long, drawn-out chess game rather than a romance. She'd pretended she had no feelings for him, but he knew that wasn't true. He'd seen right through her with those penetrating blue eyes of his, through to her very core. It used to give her a thrill every time he looked at her. It still did.

It was a relief to find she still felt the same way, now they were married. At times, the chase had seemed everything. The daring part of Mel had thrived on it. They'd had sex on Brighton pier and she'd never felt so reckless, so alive. The inner Mel, though, had craved security, and when Steve asked her to run away with him, she'd chosen to stay and marry Ian. It was the worst decision of her life, she reflected, as she stepped out of the shower cubicle and wrapped herself in a towel. She rubbed the steamed-up mirror, trying to make out her reflection. Her face, indistinct and hazy, stared back at her, droplets of condensation coursing down it. Well, I've made up for that now, she thought. It isn't everyone who gets a second chance. She decided to be lenient with him for going snorkelling without her. Marriage was supposed to be flexible, and Steve needed space to do his own thing, too. He might be a bit of an unknown quantity but, all in all, she preferred it that way.

'I can see why you'd fight shy of relationships, after that.' Delilah took her dark glasses off and looked at Steve sympathetically. 'What an ordeal.'

'It was.'

'It explains a lot about you.'

He glanced at her edgily. 'What do you mean?'

'A man of your age – what are you, mid-thirties? – getting married for the first time. It's quite late.'

'I'm choosy.'

'Or scared of the "C" word?'

'Yeah, well, once bitten and all that.'

'So you have been married before?'

He shook his head. 'No. Engaged. That was before ... it was five years ago.'

'Does Mel know?'

He shook his head.

'I won't say anything, promise.'

'It's no big secret, really. I just haven't ... I don't talk about these things much.'

'Now's your chance, then. Confession's good for the soul.'

Her choice of words spooked him. Steve was only too aware of the irony. He swallowed, his mouth suddenly dry, and had to force himself to focus on continuing the pleasantries.

'She was called Tricia. She was an MP's daughter. My mother was in ecstasies over that one. We'd only been out on about three dates before she started planning the wedding. Bought the hat, planned the flowers, rung round hotels ... '

'Too much pressure.'

'Too right. And I got all this earache about grandchildren. Me and Tricia didn't have a chance. Not that it would've worked out anyway.' He laughed dryly. 'She didn't really have "it". You know?'

'I do know,' Delilah said with feeling, looking out across the sea.

Suddenly, she leapt to her feet. 'Swing out here.' Moving with surprising agility given the amount of alcohol she'd consumed, she grabbed the tiller and hauled it across. Too late, Steve noticed a dark mass looming right in front of them, just breaking the waves. The bow inched forty-five degrees to port with agonizing slowness. They were almost on top of the rocks. Steve could see the water boiling over their hulking surface. He tensed himself for impact. Incredibly, the boat churned past without a scrape.

'Jesus.' Sweat trickled down the sides of his face from underneath the baseball cap. 'That was close.'

She waved a hand dismissively. 'My fault. I should've been watching you.'

'If you hadn't been so quick ... '

'Told you I needed a couple of bottles before I'm firing on all cylinders.' She gave him back the tiller. 'We're OK now. Just stay wide of that channel.' She pointed to a stretch of shimmering green water. 'It gets shallower there. More chance of bumping into something. This bit round the headland's always tricky.'

'Where are we?'

'Heading towards Discovery Bay.' She studied his face. 'Are you OK? You look a bit pale.'

'I'm fine.'

'Good.' She threw him another beer. 'Come on, full throttle. I'm starving.'

Feeling self-conscious and rather lonely, Mel ate a delicious lunch of tilapia snapper outside on the patio. She dismissed Dolly, telling her Steve was taking her out for dinner, and decided to put her feet up in the hammock with a good book. The hammock, a proper one, was slung between two trees in the secluded back garden. Steve had obviously adjusted it to his height and Mel clambered into it with some difficulty, floundering about like a fish. Grateful no-one could see the performance, she settled back, only to discover that the sun was shining through the leaves at such an angle it was straight in her eyes. Tutting with annoyance, she half-fell out of the hammock – it seemed the easiest way to dismount – and went back to the house for her sunglasses.

The shades were nowhere to be found. After ransacking the bedroom and emptying the contents of assorted bags all over the floor, Mel was about to give up when she remembered that she'd given them to Steve to look after at the party. What would he have done with them? She glanced at the bedside table. No sign. His jacket was draped over the back of a chair and she decided to check his pockets. There, in the breast pocket, were her precious Raybans. A piece of paper, which had been folded up, was caught around one of the arms. Curious, she took it off and opened it out. It had a figure written on it in a flamboyant hand: *IOU £100,000.*

Mel studied the paper, frowning. What did this mean? It couldn't be something old because the jacket was new, a lightweight one bought especially for the honeymoon. And the fact that the paper was caught up with the glasses suggested Steve had put it in his pocket the previous evening, at the party. She wondered what he had been discussing with Desmond Taylor. It hadn't occurred to her to ask; she'd assumed Taylor had been showing off his boat, as Delilah had suggested. Thinking about it, they had been gone a long time. That was why she'd got so drunk, waiting for him. Perhaps it was to do with a business deal, though what, Mel couldn't imagine.

She refolded the paper and put it back in his pocket. There was no point in leaping to conclusions or going off at him. Steve wouldn't be too impressed if he thought she was a snoop. She'd just have to keep a closer eye on him. Never mind giving him space; from now on she was going to watch him like a hawk.

Having second thoughts, she replaced the sunglasses too. It was best not to arouse suspicion. She chided herself for being so chary – there was bound to be a perfectly logical, legal explanation for this. It didn't mean Steve was up to anything dodgy. Look on the bright side, she comforted herself, you can go up to the hotel mall and get yourself a new pair.

Ignoring the alarm bells going off in the back of her head, she pulled on pedal pushers, pumps and a cropped top, completing the ensemble off with a fetching sun-hat. Hang the expense, she was off to buy Gucci. Steve could obviously afford it. She might even have a browse through the jewellery and watches while she was at it.

Steve and Delilah had a long and pleasant lunch in Runaway Bay at a popular local bar-cum-grill that did, indeed, serve the best seafood Steve had ever tasted. He found Delilah surprisingly good company: she was shrewd and entertaining, even if she was a lush, and she had a robust sense of humour. He had not wanted to like her, but, equally, he found it impossible to dislike her. She was nothing like Barbara Owen; rather the reverse. While Steve could think of many good reasons for hurrying the end of his sick embittered old mother, Delilah, he thought, deserved a drying-out clinic and a decent bloke, not a watery grave.

Still, he pondered, 100,000 smackers was not an amount to turn down lightly – or to turn down at all. He had plans for that money. Doug Bayliss had set him the example, and ever since the age of twenty-two, Steve had been determined to build his own empire. He had been serious when he told Delilah about starting more clubs; he'd just omitted to tell her she would be, indirectly, financing his planned expansion.

'Penny for them,' Delilah slurred, peering at him from over the top of her shades.

They had both consumed a considerable amount of alcohol, and although Steve was trying to pace himself, the beers, on top of the previous night's booze, were beginning to kick in.

'What?' he asked sleepily, rubbing his eyes. It was very hot and he was feeling slightly groggy.

'You were miles away.'

'Sorry.'

'I hope she was nice. I don't want to be blanked for just any young slapper.'

'Not she. He.'

'Ooh. Now that *does* sound interesting.' She winked. 'I'm very broad-minded, Steve.'

'It's nothing like that.' He took another swig of beer – his sixth.

'No? Then there must be money involved. Sex and money, they're at the root of most things.'

'True.' Steve looked at her, unsmiling. 'And revenge.' He savoured the word, thinking of Phil Mitchell.

Delilah appeared not to be listening. 'I used to think that love was what motivated people, one way or the other. Something purer than sex, you know? But I've seen so much greed, so much selfishness ... ' She paused, peering at a young black man standing by the bar as if she recognized him. He turned to go and her face fell. ' ... It's hard to know any more,' she continued, almost to herself.

Steve's expression was a mask. He twirled a fork over and over in his fingers like a baton, saying nothing.

Delilah appeared to snap out of her reverie. 'So which was it with this bloke?' she asked brightly. 'Money, revenge or – '

'Forget it.' Steve got up from the table.

'Are we going? I haven't finished my drink.'

'You've had enough,' he said gruffly. 'It's nearly five. I've got to get back, Mel will be worrying.'

'Well, Dessie won't.'

'You never know.' Steve pulled his baseball cap down over his brow. 'He might be.'

He crossed the road without waiting for her and strode off across the beach, heading towards the shallows where the skiff was anchored. Delilah trotted after him, stumbling in the sand and clutching at her hat, which was attempting to take off in the breeze. Without bothering to remove his shoes, Steve splashed through the water and clambered into the boat. He started the outboard engine.

'That was extremely rude,' blazed Delilah, paddling through the shallows and getting the hem of her cotton dress soaked in the process. 'And for God's sake be a gentleman and help me into this bloody boat.'

He hauled her in without ceremony and she flopped down on a seat.

'You won't get far without lifting the anchor, sailor boy,' she said waspishly.

Gritting his teeth, Steve pulled it in. They set off west out of the bay into the now lowering sun. The glare of the light off the water made it difficult to see ahead and Steve kept well out, wary of the rocks. They passed fishermen returning home, who waved and smiled. This time, Steve did not wave back.

'Would you care to tell me what I've done?' Delilah asked.

Steve set his jaw.

'Fine,' she shouted. 'If you're not going to talk to me, I'll just sit here and get drunk.'

'You are drunk.'

'You think? You ain't seen nothing yet.'

'Go ahead. I'm not stopping you.'

'No, you're not.' She opened another bottle of wine, with some difficulty. 'All I did was ask you about this bloke, whoever he is … '

'Was.'

'Was?'

'He's dead.'

'So I've put my foot in it. *Again*. Well, how was I to know?' Her face was defiant. 'Two out of two? What are the odds against that?'

He swung round, fury in his eyes. 'What are you suggesting?'

'I'm not suggesting anything.' She sipped her wine demurely. 'You've obviously seen a lot of tragedy in your life.'

'Are you taking the piss?' Steve abandoned the tiller and went over to her, thrusting his face close to hers. 'Losing Saskia was a relief, not a tragedy.' He gripped Delilah by the shoulders. She leaned back apprehensively. 'But losing Doug, that was like losing my old man, only a million times worse, because he was more like a father to me than Dad ever was. Now that *was* a tragedy.' He had Delilah pinioned against the side of the boat, holding her down. She struggled helplessly, holding on to the gunwales.

'Get off me.'

Steve ignored her. It was as if Delilah's taunt had thrown a switch in his brain, he was on autopilot, battling with some inner demon.

'You see, there are different kinds of deaths, Delilah,' he continued, staring at her but not seeing her any more. 'Some are pointless and stupid and careless. Some are awful and terrible and tear your heart out. And some – some are just tragically predictable.'

He yanked her to her feet. Delilah staggered, losing her balance, and grabbed hold of Steve's shirt to save herself. The skiff was fairly stable, but with their combined weight all on one side it began to list to starboard. Steve, pulled towards Delilah, found himself overbalancing. He reached out, but there was nothing to catch hold of.

'Step back,' she yelled, but the small boat was tipping up and up out of the water and, as if in slow motion, he was falling down and down through the air.

He heard, as if from a great distance, Delilah's scream. For an instant he seemed to hover above the deep calm sea and saw in the pond-like surface his own black shadow. It was like looking into a mirror and seeing his destiny. Then his body hit the water.

NINE

'Steve! Steve! Can you hear me?' A hand slapped his face, once, twice, three times. He twisted away to avoid the stinging blows, coughing and retching his guts up. The same rough hand rolled him over on to his side, supporting him while he vomited. 'It's OK, it's OK,' a voice repeated soothingly. He opened his eyes, seeing the floor of the boat, a puddle of water and regurgitated seafood. The hand wiped his face clean with a rag. Steve loved that hand. His bleary vision focused on it, imprinting on the chipped nail varnish, the salt-reddened skin, the bejewelled fingers. That hand had saved him.

'Do you think you can sit?' Delilah's face swung over him, round and pale as the moon. She wrapped her arms around him and hoisted him up, supporting him on her breast. He could feel her breath rasping in and out, lungs working like bellows, like his own lungs, in fact, which were gasping greedily for air. He hadn't realized the rackety noise was coming from him.

How long they sat together like that, he didn't know. Time seemed to have stopped. He seemed, somehow, to be in a different world, a world where colours and shapes and sounds and smells were immediate and intense. It was if he couldn't see the big picture any more, just lots and lots of little ones. It was, he thought, listening to Delilah's heart thudding in his ear, like being reborn.

'What happened to you, Steve? Suddenly you just went crazy.'

Steve didn't answer.

Delilah sighed heavily. 'You can't charge around in a small boat. Do you know how many people drown each year from falling overboard or capsizing? Such a waste of life. And all because they don't think.' She had cut the engine and they were drifting, as if becalmed. The cliffs looked a long way away.

Unsteadily, Steve picked himself up and groped his way to a seat. He put his head in his hands.

'Anyway, lecture over,' Delilah said. 'You're alive. That's the main thing.'

'I shouldn't be,' he said, his voice muffled. 'I don't deserve to be.'

'Don't talk nonsense.'

'It's not. It's the truth.'

'You think I should have let you drown?'

Steve was silent.

Delilah busied herself opening under-seat lockers. 'At least I didn't tip in – though how I managed to hang on, I'll never know. We're lucky the boat didn't go right over. If I'd fallen overboard, neither of us would've stood a chance. I'm a hopeless swimmer. Here.' She chucked him a towel.

'Thanks.'

'I think we've got some medicinal brandy somewhere. Yes, here it is.' She produced a hip flask and unscrewed it. 'Leave me some.'

Steve took a large swig, coughing as the fiery spirit seared his throat. Wiping his watering eyes he passed it back to Delilah.

'Better?'

'A bit.'

She took a swig herself, sighing with satisfaction. 'You didn't answer my question.'

'Which one?'

'Come on, Steve. Don't play me for a fool. What's going on?'

'You really want to know?'

'Yes, I do.'

'Your husband has hired me to kill you.'

She drew a deep breath. 'And is that what you were trying to do just now?'

'I don't know.'

'I see,' Delilah said coolly. She checked her watch. The sun was low now, colouring both the sky and the sea a spectacular red, as if the waves themselves were being flambéed. She stood up, causing the boat to rock, and looked him straight in the eye. 'It will be getting dark soon. If you're going to have another go, you'd better do it now.'

By early evening Steve still hadn't returned. Mel had changed into a (newly acquired) frock and put up her hair, ready to go out, but as the minutes ticked by she grew increasingly anxious and abandoned her book to sit by the open window. She had a knot in the pit of her stomach that wouldn't go away, no matter how sternly she reprimanded herself for being silly. The sensible voice that said (in her mother's brisk, no-nonsense tone), 'He's a grown man, what harm could he have come to?' was always answered by her own, scared, small-child's voice, 'He went snorkelling. He could have drowned.'

Tortured by scenarios of Steve floating face down in the sea, and unable to bear the waiting any longer, she locked the villa and went down the path to the beach to look for him.

It was already dusk, and in the fading light Mel made out a number of small boats pulled up on the shore. Hobbled by her stilettos, she wrenched them off and ran across the soft sand to where their Jamaican owners were standing around talking and drinking beer.

'Excuse me,' she panted, flustered, 'but has anyone here taken people out snorkelling today?'

The group of men burst out laughing.

'We all have,' one of them explained, adding, 'You want to go now? I take you. No problem.' He looked her up and down appreciatively. 'Only you won't see much in the dark. Me have to swim wit' you.' The others laughed and whistled.

'I don't want to go out,' Mel answered crossly. 'I'm looking for my husband. He went out snorkelling this morning and he's not come back. Are there any other boats still out?'

They conferred among themselves.

'Everyone is here,' another, older man supplied. 'But your husband could have come back earlier. Maybe him in a bar.'

She smiled half-heartedly. 'If he's in a bar, I'm going to kill him.'

'What does your husband look like?' the man asked sympathetically.

'He's English, his name's Steve, he's thirty-five, tall, slim, good-looking – ' this evoked more cheers and whistles ' – dark hair, sort of swept back, and blue eyes. *Very* blue eyes.' She scanned their faces expectantly, but none of them seemed to recognize the description.

'If he's that handsome, then me *sure* him in a bar,' the older man said. 'Don't you worry your head. Him be back soon. No problem.'

'Thank you,' Mel replied, drooping slightly. Somehow, she did not share their confidence.

She made her way over to the jetty, noticing, as she got closer, a man standing at the end of it, hands in pockets. His broad shoulders and thick neck looked familiar. As she drew closer, she realized it was Desmond Taylor. He looked as if he was waiting for someone.

Taylor must have caught the vibration of her tread on the springy planks – Mel was still shoeless – because he swung round.

'Is that Melanie – or am I just hallucinating this vision of loveliness before me?' he cackled, switching immediately from pensive to expansive mode.

'Depends what you've been taking,' she said dryly.

'Not enough to dull my senses.' He raised a tumbler to her. 'You are flesh and blood and you are utterly gorgeous.'

'Um, thanks.' She disengaged herself from his slobbery, whisky-laden kiss. 'What are you doing here?' She caught him looking at her oddly and the knot in her stomach tightened.

'The same thing as you, I suspect. Waiting for my good lady and your husband. I'm beginning to think they must have sailed off into the sunset together.' He laughed loudly. 'Tell you what, if they have, how's about you and me shacking up, eh?'

'But Steve left me a note to say he was going snorkelling,' she said, puzzled, refusing to grace his offer with a response. Desmond Taylor, she decided, was the sort of man who would automatically proposition any remotely attractive female.

'Did he? Well, I expect that's what he was planning to do before Del buttonholed him. She can be very persuasive, that woman. It takes a strong man to say no to her. I can't.' Taylor's conviviality sounded a little strained. He downed the dregs of his whisky. 'Actually, I think Steve did say something about snorkelling, now you mention it. That was when Del said he could do it from our boat.'

'Shouldn't they be back by now, though? I mean, you're obviously worried, too.'

'Me? Worried? Nah.' He put an arm around her shoulders. 'I was just taking the air and thought I'd have a little look, see if they're back, that's all. I expect they've stopped off somewhere. I'll get a ring on the mobile soon, I betcha.'

'And if you don't?' There was a tremor in Mel's voice.

Taylor checked his watch. 'We'll give 'em another couple of hours. If they're not back by then, we'll send out a search party. But it won't come to that, I promise you, love.' He gave her another squeeze. 'Come on up to the house and I'll get you a stiff one. I'll post one of the lads here to keep a watch.'

Mel felt a lump form in her throat. She swallowed hard. 'I'd better not. Steve won't know where I am.'

Taylor scratched his head. 'It's gonna be dark, soon, love. I don't like the thought of you sitting out here all by yourself. Besides, you're gonna ruin that beautiful frock – and I know how much it cost, cos we sell 'em up the mall.' He winked. 'I shall have words with that Steve when he gets back, leaving you all dressed up and nowhere to go.'

'But that's what I mean. Steve wouldn't do that.'

He squinted out to sea, screwing his eyes up against the glare of the setting sun. 'You know what?' he said, turning to her. 'I bet Del's persuaded him to go ashore, take her for dinner somewhere. They'll probably leave the boat behind and come back by taxi. She's done that before.' Taylor sighed heavily. 'Then I'll have to send Francis and a boy out to bring the bloody thing back tomorrow.'

'Oh. You think that's possible?'

'More than possible. Once she's got her claws into a good-lookin' fella, she hangs on for dear life – not that she's any competition for you, darlin'. Let's just say she likes to make the most of opportunities. All that flirting and carrying on, it don't mean nothing, it's a way of getting her own back on me. Tell you the truth, things ain't that good between us, Melanie. But I expect she told you that.'

'She did say something.'

He shrugged. 'So you know I ain't no saint. I admit it. And this dragging it out with Steve, it's just a wind-up, see? Nothing personal against you.'

Mel scowled. 'Well, she's got a funny way of showing it. Anyway, I'm still not convinced. Steve's not the type to be browbeaten.'

'Yeah, I know that, but he ain't a sailor, either, is he? Del's probably had a skinful, so she'll be out of it. And it's very easy to lose track of time and then find you ain't got enough daylight left to make it home safely. He ain't gonna risk coming back by boat in the dark, is he? Not if he's got any sense.'

'No, I suppose not.'

'There you go then. Now, why don't you wait at the villa, cos if Steve turns up in a taxi and you're not there, this thing could go on all night. I'll keep a fella here, like I said, and I'll ring you as soon as I hear from them. Which I expect to be very shortly. OK?'

'OK,' Mel agreed.

Taylor's explanations all sounded perfectly reasonable, but for some reason she couldn't put her finger on, she wasn't entirely sure she believed him. Still, there didn't seem to be much else she could do.

Steve's journey had indeed been a race against time to get back before nightfall, a race that, in the last twenty minutes, he had lost. He discovered a couple of lanterns stowed away and hung them over the bow, but they were no use for illuminating the way ahead. He comforted himself that at least on-coming ships would be able to see him – pleasure boats offering 'Sunset Cruises' were popular around Montego Bay – and hoped that the starlight would be sufficient for him to navigate by.

His eyes had grown accustomed to the dark, and he could make out the outline of the cliffs clearly enough, but he was worried about running into hidden rocks. There was no Delilah to help him now. Another worry was that he might actually sail right past Crescent Beach, heading too far west. He did not know how much fuel he had left and the thought of the outboard motor cutting out in the middle of the protected Montego Bay Marine Park, the stretch of coastline edging Sangster International Airport, was not propitious.

Still, these were risks he had weighed up and decided to take, Steve told himself. All in all, he was confident he had made the right decision. It was worth facing a bit of danger to net that kind of cash. Anyway, he had already cheated death twice today, counting the near miss with the rocks. A third time would be very, very unlucky indeed. The fact that he had survived the fall overboard had made him unexpectedly gung-ho. So what if he was, literally, plunging into the dark? Steve felt himself grinning stupidly, a great big sappy smile. This was exhilarating. Buoyed up with adrenalin, he powered on in the little boat. It was great to be alive.

He need not have worried about overshooting the bay. The string of coloured lights decorating the jetty had been switched on again, enabling Steve to pick out Crescent Beach easily.

He suspected this might have something to do with Taylor, and so it proved.

Desmond Taylor was waiting anxiously for him as Steve cut the engine and glided silently into the shallows. The boat ran aground with a bump, making him lurch forward. He climbed out with wobbly legs, feeling the cold water fill his shoes, and watched Taylor jog towards him. Puffing and blowing, Taylor stopped at the edge of the water. He stared at the empty boat but said nothing.

'Give me a hand to pull her up,' Steve said nonchalantly, throwing him the rope.

Taylor complied, still not speaking. They dragged *Delilah Too* – all of a sudden, the name seemed desperately ironic – to where the other small boats were lined up higher on the beach.

Taylor mopped his forehead. 'Clever, coming in under cover of darkness. I didn't think you'd have the balls.' He peered inside the boat, as if perhaps expecting to see Delilah curled up on the floor. 'I see you have bigger *cajones* than I thought.' He gripped the side of the boat with both hands, hanging his head, his eyes screwed tight shut. When he looked back up, his eyes glittered in the watery moonlight. 'So. It's done.' He dashed his cheeks with a bear-like paw. 'I can hardly believe it.'

'Get over it, Desmond. You're a free man. Delilah won't be bothering you any more,' Steve said curtly.

The tears were running freely down Taylor's face now. 'Give us a moment alone, will you?' he asked.

'Sure,' Steve said, raising his hand. 'Take as long as you like.'

He walked away towards the palms. Looking back over his shoulder, he saw Desmond Taylor on his knees in the sand. He appeared to be praying. Whether is was for deliverance or whether he was giving thanks, Steve couldn't be sure.

'You're a man of your word, Steve,' Taylor said, rejoining him five minutes later. 'And so am I. Come up to the big house and we'll sort out what we discussed this morning.'

'OK,' Steve replied, 'but I've got to find Mel first. She'll be wondering where I've got to.'

'You got a bulletproof vest under that T-shirt?' Taylor joked. 'Cos I think you're gonna need one.'

Steve winced. 'I left her a note saying I'd take her out to dinner.'

'I think she'll be happy you're back in one piece. She was out here, waiting for you.'

'What did you tell her?'

'That you and Del had gone out in the boat. Might as well keep the story as near to the truth as possible, eh? Less chance of slipping up.'

'So what am I going to tell her about Delilah?'

'The truth, I guess. Sooner people know there's been an accident, the better.' Taylor paused. 'Bring her up to the house. I gotta be at this function, you can find me there and break the sad news.' He clapped Steve on the back and started to walk away, then turned round again. 'Delilah ... she didn't suffer, did she?'

'I promise you, mate,' Steve replied, 'she didn't feel a thing.'

'Thank you, Steve. That is a great consolation to me.' He continued on his way with a jauntiness of step that belied his sombre expression.

Steve watched him go, his lip curled in scorn. Bracing himself, he set off to face Mel.

He had hardly got both feet inside the door when Mel let him have both barrels.

'You had better have a very, *very* good explanation for where you've been.' Her voice shook with anger. She stood in front of Steve, arms folded. 'Well?'

'I'm sorry, sweetheart.' He reached out to hold her, but she shrugged him off furiously. 'Look, things got a bit complicated with Delilah. I've had one hell of a day.' He rubbed his eyes wearily. 'I know you've been worried, and I'm sorry, but can we do this later? I need a hot shower, a hot coffee and a change of clothes before I do anything.'

'Did she come on to you? Desmond said she likes making a play for other blokes.'

'It was a bit more complicated than that.'

'Steve!' Mel exploded. 'Why can't you ever give me a straight answer? I'm fed up with being excluded. Just tell me.'

'I will, *I will*. After I've told Desmond. It's only right he should be the first to know.'

'What are you on about?' She looked at him closely. 'You're scaring me. Did something happen? Steve? *Steve*!'

The maître d' told Steve that Desmond Taylor was addressing members of the Montego Bay Yacht Club and could not be interrupted.

'He'll want to hear this,' Steve said. 'Tell him it's urgent. It's about his wife.'

Marking the steely glint in his eye, the maître d' stalked off.

Steve turned to Mel. 'Look, sweetheart, I'd better do this privately. I'll meet you in the bar, all right?'

'Are you sure you don't me there for want moral support?'

'No, I'll manage.' He pecked her cheek. 'Off you go.'

She departed, glancing back over her shoulder at him, her face anxious. He caught the look and smiled reassuringly.

The maître d' returned a few minutes later. 'Monsieur Taylor will see you now,' he conceded, as if granting an audience with royalty.

Steve followed him through a door marked 'Staff Only' and down a corridor to a room which he assumed must be Taylor's office. The maître d' rapped on the door rather officiously, then stood aside to let Steve enter. Taylor was seated behind a large desk, glass of red wine in hand.

'Steve! Come in, mate,' he boomed. 'Thank you, Antoine.'

The maître d' gave a courteous bow and retreated, shutting the door.

'Takes his job very seriously, does Antoine,' Taylor confided. 'Bloody head waiters; always think they run the show. He's French,' he added, as if that explained everything.

'Let's cut the crap, shall we?' Steve said impatiently.

'Brass tacks, eh?' Taylor took a sip of wine. 'All right then. Give me the details of where it happened, then I'll phone the coastguard and we'll set the wheels in motion. Best to do it all by the book.' He chewed his lip thoughtfully. 'You did see her go under, didn't you, Steve? There ain't no chance they'll fish her out alive, is there?'

'None.' Steve regarded him levelly. 'Delilah's long gone. I like to think she's in a happier place now.'

'Now that's a nice way of putting it. I'll try and remember to use that meself,' Taylor cackled. 'It's true enough, bleedin' cow was always a right misery guts when she was alive.'

'Yeah, she told me how unhappy she was with her life. I think that's why she was so co-operative, when it came to it.'

'Co-operative?' Taylor almost fell out of his chair. 'Whaddya mean? The old girl jumped overboard all by herself?'

'Oh, she jumped all right,' Steve said, smiling. 'Into her boyfriend's boat.'

Taylor stood up, his face thunderous. 'What kind of cobblers is this? She ain't got a boyfriend. If you ain't gone through with our agreement – '

'Sit down,' Steve said coldly. 'I don't think you're in any position to dictate terms, Desmond. Arranging to have your wife murdered is a criminal offence.'

'Who's gonna believe you? It's your word against mine.'

'True,' Steve said. 'Though of course you don't know which way Sophie would go, do you? If the pressure was on. Especially if she wasn't getting her blood money. She seemed pretty flexible when we were alone together. I'd watch her, if I was you.'

'How dare you suggest that about my Sophie!' Taylor went puce.

'Your Sophie wanted me to pop you after I'd done Delilah. Once she'd married you, of course.' Steve shrugged. 'I didn't take her seriously. I think she was just offering a little incentive. She didn't like being... turned down.'

Taylor sank back into his seat, looking dazed. 'You're making this up.'

'Believe what you like.' Steve stuffed his hands into his pockets. 'As it happens, I don't fancy dragging the law into it, Desmond. It ain't my style. As you would know, from talking to my mate Tony Sheen.' He paused, absent-mindedly examining a painting on the wall. 'Tony and I go back a long way. I expect he told you that. He's gone up in the world now from when we used to work together. He's got friends in very high places.' He turned back to Taylor. 'Well, "friends" is one word for them.'

'Are you threatening me?'

'Tony told me you owed him a favour. "*A bloody big favour*" were the words he used. This holiday was supposed to be his wedding present to us. He won't be too impressed with you when he gets my postcard.' Steve put his hands on Taylor's desk, leaning towards him threateningly. 'I'd say it was my turn to tell you the deal.'

TEN

'Where's Delilah? I don't buy all this stuff about a boyfriend for one minute. You two have cooked something up together, haven't you? Jesus!' Taylor thumped the desk with his fist, scattering a pot of paper clips. 'What's it gonna be, Steve? Blackmail? Is that the game you're playing now?' He gave a hollow laugh. 'That'd be right. I even planted the idea, didn't I? Come on then, let's hear it. What's your price?'

'I learned a valuable lesson today, Desmond.' Steve reached slowly into his breast pocket. 'When you're looking death in the face, money becomes meaningless. No matter how much you thought you wanted it, or needed it. Suddenly you get a whole new perspective on life. Know what I mean?' He withdrew his hand. There was a gun in it. Taylor froze. 'Delilah taught me that. That was when we reached our ... understanding,' Steve continued. 'I was the one that almost drowned. She saved me. And for that, I owe her a debt that not even you, Desmond, with all your millions, can ever repay.' He extended his arm, pointing the gun at him unwaveringly. 'I told her that. And do you know what she said?' He smiled nastily. 'She said, "That bastard was going to have you kill me. Let's see how he likes it when the tables are turned." Steve stepped around the desk, still aiming the revolver at Taylor's head. 'What's a bloke to do, eh? A promise is a promise.' He jabbed the muzzle of the gun in Taylor's shoulder blades. '"Live now, pay later." That's your motto, ain't it?'

'Yes,' he croaked.

'And what did I say to you, Desmond?'

'Um ... "What if you have to pay now?".'

'That's right.' Steve gave him another prod with the gun. 'Which is how it goes sometimes in this world.'

'*Please* don't shoot me, Steve,' Taylor pleaded. 'Steve, *please* mate. I'll give you anything ... ' His sweat was rank, soaking through his expensive shirt in large wet patches. He tried to turn to look at him, but Steve pushed him roughly. 'Keep facing forwards.'

'The safe's behind you. I'll give you the combination.'

Steve put his mouth close to Taylor's ear. 'Still don't get it, do you, Desmond? That's not the kind of payment Delilah had in mind.' He saw Taylor's shoulders shake, and realized he was crying silently. 'I bet she's sorry she ain't here to see this. She said she wanted me to blow your brains out.' He moved the gun slowly up Taylor's back and pressed it against the side of his head. 'That's what she wanted. She was one very angry woman.'

Steve paused, dragging the moment out. Taylor started to whimper. 'But, unlike you, Desmond, she ain't sick enough to go through with such a thing. Which doesn't mean I ain't. As you know. I'm pretty handy with a shooter, though I say it myself.'

'*Please*, I'm *begging* you, *please* don't ... '

Steve looked at the blubbering man with disgust. He dropped his voice to a whisper. 'However, sometimes it's enough just to give someone a taste of their own medicine. I should know. It's been done to me. And I can tell you, the effect lasts longer.' He straightened up abruptly, throwing the gun on the desk with a clatter. Taylor jerked backwards instinctively. 'Anyway, I told her this thing wouldn't pop a weasel. Let alone a rat like you.'

'It's not real?' Taylor quavered.

'Nah, it's a kid's toy. I borrowed it off Delilah's boyfriend's brother. He's got two little boys. They're into all that "bang bang you're dead" stuff. Held me up the minute we walked in the room. That's what gave me the idea.'

'I – I – I don't know what to say.' Taylor slumped forward. 'I thought you were really gonna do it.' He rubbed his eyes. 'What kind of twisted bastard are you?'

'Funny. Sophie said the same thing.'

Taylor got unsteadily to his feet. 'What have you done to her? You 'aven't hurt her, have you?'

'Like I said, Desmond. It's what I didn't do that upset your girlfriend.'

Taylor launched himself at Steve with a roar, knocking him flying. With his height and bulk he overpowered him with little trouble. Steve struggled to escape, but Taylor had him pinned down and landed a punishing blow to the face, followed by two more in rapid succession. Blood spattered on to the pale carpet. Steve cried out in pain.

'Not so clever now, are we?' Taylor said, panting.

'Hitting me might make you feel better, but it ain't gonna solve your problems,' Steve gasped, his nose pouring. 'Delilah's expecting my call. If she doesn't hear from me, she's gonna hit you. With everything. And I mean, everything.'

'What do you mean by that?'

'She ain't daft. She knows how you made your fortune. She's kept her mouth shut all these years because it was in her own interest. Well, not any more.'

Taylor let him go. Steve crawled on to all fours, reaching for a handkerchief to stem the bleeding. He got up slowly, supporting himself on a chair. One eye was rapidly closing, there was a red mark on his cheek and his lip had been cut. The two men stared at each other, breathing hard. Steve was the one to break the deadlock.

'I'd say we're back to square one. Wouldn't you?' Holding the bloody handkerchief to his nose, he said, 'Now, are you gonna break out that Scotch of yours, because I for one could do with a glass.' Spotting a refrigerated cabinet in the corner – Taylor obviously liked to have cold beer on tap – he added, 'And I hope you've got plenty of ice in that thing.'

Taylor seemed to shake himself, as if readjusting. 'Frozen peas, that's what you need. I'll get the kitchen to send a couple of packets up.'

He reached for the phone, but Steve moved swiftly, ripping the cord out before he could dial the number.

'No third parties, Desmond.' He locked the office door. 'We're gonna hammer this out between us. And I ain't leaving until it's sorted. OK?'

Mel was on her third gin and tonic, knocking them back too fast on an empty stomach. She was beginning to feel strangely light-headed, as if she wasn't really there. It was a feeling she fully intended to cultivate. After the worry of waiting for Steve, the things he'd told her when he did, finally, show up, had freaked her out completely.

Chief among them was the horrific image of him falling overboard and almost drowning. She had felt in her gut that something had happened, and the knowledge that she'd been right was no consolation.

The second disturbing revelation was that Delilah had absconded with a young fisherman and somehow managed to make Steve an accessory to this. Once she had got over the initial surprise, the idea of the fifty-year-old Delilah having a Jamaican toyboy didn't seem so very far-fetched – based on the evidence of the party, there was plenty of life left in her – but just how it implicated Steve with Desmond Taylor, she wasn't sure. That, presumably, was what the pair of them were discussing right now. Niggling away at the back of her mind was the figure of £100,000 written on the paper in Steve's pocket. Mel hadn't had a chance to broach this, and this evening was clearly not a good time. Still, she couldn't help wondering whether the sum of money and Delilah's disappearance were linked. The subject raised such a quagmire of suspicions that Mel didn't know where to start. Better to get drunk, she decided.

She had just ordered her fourth G&T when a stunning brunette walked into the bar, making the kind of entrance that even Mel had to grudgingly admire. There was no shortage of stunning women at the Crescent Beach Club – it was a favourite with beautiful people the world over – but even among the resort's A-list guests, the brunette stood out. She surveyed the room, hand on hip, with a model's hauteur, and then, to Mel's astonishment, walked over to her.

'You look like a girl that's been stood up as well,' she drawled in an upper-class English accent.

'Not stood up. Abandoned. For the second time today.' Mel waved her glass. 'I'm drowning my sorrows.'

'Mind if I join you?'

'Feel free.' Mel glanced around. 'Although every man in this room is on the starting blocks to buy you a drink.'

'Oh, I don't need to pay,' the brunette said airily. 'My boyfriend runs the place. I put them on his tab.'

'But Desmond Taylor is the owner,' Mel said, puzzled.

'Yeah, Dessie. That's my fella.' She hailed a bartender. 'I'll have my usual.'

Mel's jaw dropped. 'You're – I mean, I've heard about you. Well, you know how people gossip,' she added tipsily.

'Don't I.' The brunette yawned delicately. 'It doesn't bother me. I don't care what they think. All I can say is, their own lives must be desperately dull.' She raised her glass. 'Cheers. I'm Sophie.'

'Mel.'

Sophie appraised her unashamedly. 'Are you a model, too? No, you're too old. Actress, perhaps?'

'Oh, no. Nothing like that,' Mel said, smarting. 'I'm a barmaid, actually. And, like you, I don't care what people think.'

Sophie raised her arched eyebrows. 'No need to be touchy. Though I'm surprised you can afford the Crescent on a barmaid's wages. Or aren't you having to pay?'

'Unlike you, Sophie, I don't prostitute myself with a married sugar daddy. I'm here on my honeymoon.'

'And your husband's deserted you already? Shame on him.'

'I trust him.' Mel's acknowledgement was frosty. 'Which is more than can be said for Desmond.'

'I see.' Sophie narrowed her green eyes. 'You're in *her* camp, are you?' She pretended boredom. 'Frankly I can't see how that alcoholic old tart has any supporters. She makes poor Dessie's life hell.'

'Not any more,' Mel retaliated. 'She's left him.'

'Left him?' Sophie's languor was instantly forgotten. 'What do you mean? How do you know?'

'I know,' slurred Mel, 'because she talked my husband into helping her get away. He says she's shacked up with a boyfriend half her age. Good for her, I say.' She raised her glass in an ironic toast. Sophie looked as if she was going to explode. 'I should've thought you'd be pleased,' Mel bitched. 'Leaves the door open for you, doesn't it?' She started to hum the 'Bridal March'.

'She'll take him for half of everything.' Sophie screeched. 'What's so bloody good about that?' She recovered herself sufficiently to ask, 'Anyway, how did your husband get involved?'

'I think he just happened to be in the right place at the right time,' Mel said thoughtfully.

Steve's head ached and his cheek was throbbing, but the whisky was doing a good job of numbing the pain. The bleeding had stopped, and he had cleaned himself up as best he could with wet tissues, but his eye was purple and his lip swollen. Together with the bloody shirt, it gave him a kind of gangster cred that seemed to impress Taylor, particularly as Steve gave no indication that he was suffering. A certain amount of honour had been restored by the fight, and they were now facing each other across the desk on businesslike terms. As Taylor put it, 'You put the frighteners on me, I punched your lights out. I reckon that makes us about equal.' He was a man who made a quick recovery.

'So let me get this straight,' Taylor was saying. 'You're telling me that Del's been seeing this guy who's dirt poor, lives with his brother's family and makes his living from fishing?' He shook his head in disbelief. 'She was harping on about the simple life, but Jeez, I never saw that one coming.'

'She doesn't see things like that. Apparently he's young, sexy, fun to be with and totally devoted to her.'

'To her money, more like.' Taylor pursed his lips. 'I'd like to see how long this lasts when he finds out what she's asking for.'

'Delilah thinks having money ruins relationships. That's why she's letting you off so lightly. You've got to admit, you're gonna walk out of this smelling of roses.'

'I've gotta live with the humiliation of the whole island knowing Desmond Taylor's wife's left him for a fisherman. That's gonna do my reputation no end of good, ain't it? Bleedin' cow's rubbing me nose in it.'

'I think you should count yourself lucky, mate. All things considered.' Steve gave him a piercing look.

Taylor caught the meaning and flinched. 'I suppose it could be worse.'

'Much.'

'Yeah, all right, point taken. Run the deal by me again; it sounds too good to be true to me. She's gotta be scheming something bigger.'

'If she is, she ain't told me. What I agreed with her was simple: you put a price on her head, Desmond – £200,000, with the cash value of the holidays thrown in. Yeah?'

'Yeah,' he said reluctantly.

'And that's the money she takes from you. The cost of setting yourself free, if you like. Minus the murder rap. I'd call it a bargain.'

'And that's all?'

'She said something about negotiating a small monthly

allowance. And keeping the motor boat. But she ain't gonna fight you for your fortune.'

'Say I believe her – and I ain't saying I do – what's in it for you, Steve? I notice you omitted to mention that little detail.'

Steve looked him in the eye. 'I want what you originally offered me, £50,000. Call it twenty-five per cent commission, if it makes it sound better.' He grinned. 'A solicitor would have cost you a lot more.'

'That puts my total payout up to a quarter of a million!'

'It's peanuts for you, and you know it.'

Taylor brooded over his whisky. Finally, he said, 'Are you a gambling man, Steve?'

'Depends what the odds are.'

'Oh, I think you'll like these.' He grinned. 'Did you know about my private casino here? Gambling's illegal in Jamaica – apart from the old slot machines – but the kind of high rollers we get here, they gotta have somewhere to fritter their money away. And to be honest, there's a few locals use the place as well. It's pretty much an open secret. The authorities don't bother me.' He guffawed. 'They'd have nowhere to go if they did.' He got up. 'Come and have a look. I'll show you on the cameras, through here.'

Steve followed him through an inner door and into another suite of offices. One of them housed a bank of screens, which were being monitored by a security guard.

'You have got one on the golf course!' Steve couldn't help laughing.

Taylor looked unabashed. 'Told you I needed to keep abreast of the form.' He pointed out the pictures from the casino. It was a professional-looking set-up with uniformed croupiers running roulette tables, blackjack, craps, keno and baccarat. The casino was packed with glamorous women and men in evening dress and looked very lively.

'Impressive. Whereabouts is it?' Steve asked.

Taylor winked. 'I'll tell you – when we've finished our discussion.' He led him back to his office. 'Let me put my cards on the table, so to speak.' He poured them both more whisky. 'Fifty grand's a lotta money, Steve. Especially when you didn't carry out the work. And on top of what I've gotta now pay Del – which was gonna be zero, originally. Now let me finish,' he said, holding up his hand, as Steve opened his mouth to interrupt. 'I mean, how do I know she wasn't just gonna do this moonlight flit anyway, eh? They must've been planning it; she was obviously just waiting for the right moment. And from what you've been telling me about how she hates my money, she might not even have asked for the two hundred K.'

'She doesn't want to live in a shack, Desmond. Even Delilah ain't gonna take the simple life that far. She wants to buy a house, furnish it, set themselves up so they're comfortable ... I reckon she'd have come up with a similar figure.'

'Maybe. Maybe not. Then there's this "allowance", however much that's gonna be. I tell you, Steve, when Del says "small" that can mean anything from ten dollars to 10,000 dollars. She's got no idea about the cost of living.'

'It'll still be cheaper than taking half of everything you own.'

'Granted. But let's look at what you really did, eh? You went for a boat ride with my wife. She buggered off. You came home again. That's about the size of it.'

'You're forgetting something, ain't you? I didn't kill her. Don't tell me you aren't just a little bit glad about that?'

'Well ... perhaps.' Taylor picked up a framed family photograph off a shelf and stared at it. 'We've been through a lot, me and Del. Shame we lost it all, in the end. We don't like each other no more, but I suppose you're right – I'd feel bad with her death on my conscience. Especially as Sophie ... ' He turned away from Steve. 'It wasn't my idea, you know. She suggested it. She knows just how to get round me ... '

'Surprise, surprise.'

'I suppose you think I'm a sad old geezer who'll do anything to get his end away with a beautiful young girl.'

'You ain't the first – and you won't be the last, either. Women have made monkeys out of most of us.' He flexed his fingers, contemplating Phil Mitchell.

'I've made such a bleedin' idiot of meself.' Taylor screwed up his face. 'I knew she loved the lifestyle – I'm not that gaga – but I thought she loved me, too. I had these visions of her and me, married, swanning off around the world ... It was like being given a fresh chance, you know?' He shook his head. 'Instead I get stung by the oldest trick in the book.'

'Sex and money. They're at the root of most things. As your

wife pointed out to me,' Steve said briskly. 'Talking of which – where did we get to on my commission?'

'Ah. Well now.' Taylor sat down at his desk. 'Given the view I've just outlined, you wouldn't expect me to pay you the full whack, would you? However,' he continued hastily, 'I do appreciate your intervention – such as it was – and I am prepared to make suitable recompense.'

'How much?'

'Ten per cent.'

Steve took a step towards him. 'Are you taking the mick? Do you want me to get Tony Sheen on the blower right now and tell him about the pantomime you've put me through?'

'No, mate, no. You didn't let me finish. I'll make it ten per cent, with the chance to double or even treble it – maybe more, if you play your cards right.' He laughed. 'That's a good one.'

'What exactly are you suggesting?'

'Look, Steve. I've been a gambler all me life. A well-informed gambler, as you might say.' He tapped his nose. 'Brinkmanship. That's what I used to specialize in. Taking risks. It's how I got all this.' He spread his arms out. 'And I'd do it all again tomorrow, if I had to.'

'Get to the point, Desmond. My patience is wearing a bit thin.'

'I'll give you the money – in chips. To play at my casino. You've got – what? – five or six days left? Think of the fun you and Mel could have. Not to mention the money you could make! Whatever it is, I'll honour it, I promise you. I'll even set you up with an offshore account, just so as the taxman can't get his hands on your winnings. And, just to show it's a genuine offer, whatever chips you don't play, I'll cash in for you on the last day. I can't say fairer than that.' He rubbed his hands together. 'So, are you in?'

Steve looked at him with narrowed eyes. 'Twenty thousand in chips?'

'And you could leave here with £100,000. More, even.'

'Odds are always on the side of the house, any fool knows that.'

'True. You don't need to play at all, if you don't want to. I'll cash in the whole twenty grand if you hang on to it 'til the end. But it's gotta be worth taking a chance on, ain't it?'

Steve got up and paced the room. He did not reply.

'Come on, Steve. How're you gonna live your life? You want the prize, you gotta take the risks that go with it. That's how the big boys play. I told you that the day we met.'

Steve stopped pacing and stood in front of him. 'OK. I'll take the deal.'

Taylor pumped his hand. 'Good man.'

'I'd better go. Mel will be about to divorce me.' Steve's words were almost drowned out by a thunderous knocking on the outer door.

'Desmond! I know you're in there. I want to talk to you right this minute.'

'Sounds like your girlfriend ain't too happy,' he remarked.

'Yeah, well, that makes two of us,' Taylor said, his face darkening.

'I'll leave you to it.'

Steve opened the door, and Sophie, who had been leaning on it, almost fell into his arms. 'You!' she spat furiously. 'I might have known you'd be behind this.'

'A word of warning,' Steve whispered in her ear. 'He's on to you.'

'I don't know what you're talking about,' she pouted.

'Come in, Sophie. I want us to have a little chat,' Taylor said, rolling up his sleeves.

Mel and Steve slept in late the next morning. Dolly brought them breakfast in bed, clucking with concern at the sight of Steve's face.

'You just ring the bell if you want more coffee or anything,' she said. 'Me go and get you a steak for that poor eye.' She bustled out again, and could be heard informing Serena volubly of Steve's condition.

Mel giggled. 'I think you're going to get the full treatment from Dolly. I wouldn't be surprised if she didn't whip up one of her herbal mixtures for you.'

Steve shuddered. 'In that case, we'd better escape to the beach.'

'Sounds good to me.' She stroked his face gently. 'How do you feel now?'

'A bit battered and bruised, but I'll live.'

'I can't believe Desmond went off at you like that. It wasn't your fault Delilah left him. From what you told me, she set the whole thing up.'

'It was a big shock. He was upset and he took it out on the messenger. He did apologize afterwards.'

'I should think so.'

'Look, he said he'd make it up to me. He's offered us unrestricted use of his private casino. D'you fancy that?'

'A casino? Where?'

'In a secret basement room. Apparently, only the select few get to know about it. I had a look – it's the business.'

'Yeah, alright. I suppose we can afford to indulge ourselves, seeing as we've hardly had to spend any money.'

'That's what I thought.' He grinned. 'We'll go tonight, then.'

They spent the rest of the day relaxing on the beach, lying supine under the cloudless blue sky and retreating to the shade of the palms when the sun became too intense. Mel went swimming in the sea, although Steve could not bring himself to go in the water. The memory of what it had felt like when the waves closed over his head and his body had continued to plummet down and down into the depths as if it would go on for ever, was still far too vivid.

Looking up at the gigantic fronds of a coconut palm above him, Steve was relieved he hadn't committed Delilah to that awful fate. Even when he'd gone over to her, tipping the boat up, he hadn't actually been intending to do it. At least, he didn't think so. It was all a bit hazy: she'd touched a nerve with her comments about Doug and he'd lost it completely. That was why he never talked to anybody about Doug, or even allowed himself to think about him. The subject was just too painful. There was some stuff he hadn't even told Jackie: he couldn't bear her to be tortured with the doubts and recriminations he carried around inside him.

Not that anyone would ever know the exact truth about what happened that night in Romford in 1993. In a way, Steve thought, it was the uncertainty that plagued him the most. It was painful to remember, but Doug's ghost had been evoked and he knew that, if he was to have any hope of coming to terms with what happened, even now, eight years on, he had to revisit the past.

He remembered the scene as if it were yesterday. Doug had visited the club to go over some paperwork with him. The club was flourishing and he had been pleased with the books, congratulating Steve on doing a good job. They were having a drink at the bar afterwards when a commotion broke out on the dance floor. Typically, Doug, the big man, had waded in, without waiting for Steve to call security. Steve had gone in after Doug, as much to protect him – the fight was a vicious one and a knife blade flashed disjointedly in the strobes.

The staccato white light broke up the images of what happened next, giving the jerky movements a sense of unreality, as if it was an old-fashioned cine film, or an action sequence on a stage. Punches had been thrown left and right – Steve had felt his fist connect with someone's head at least once – and by the time the music stopped and the house lights were brought up, one of the lads was lying unconscious on the floor and Doug, as if caught out in some macabre party game, was kneeling over him, fist raised.

To this day, Steve didn't know whether it was himself or Doug that had struck the fatal blow. The strobe lighting had made it almost impossible for witnesses to see what had happened, and, when the police arrived, Doug had volunteered that he'd punched the victim before Steve could say anything. Steve was convinced Doug was covering for him and had later gone to the police station to own up to his part in it, but when the arresting officer informed him that the boy had died in hospital, he had thought better of it. Doug had pleaded guilty to manslaughter and was sentenced to ten years' imprisonment.

Steve had visited Doug frequently in prison – Doug was the cornerstone of their little family and both Steve and Jackie were bereft without him – and was shocked at the change in him within a few short weeks. Even now he cringed at the memory of his last visit, seeing the once hulking Doug, who had always been the epitome of rude health, so silent and desiccated and shrunken. Two days later, Doug had hung himself in his cell. A heartbroken Jackie ran away to nurse her grief alone and Steve was left with the burden of knowing that he might have set the events into motion that led to Doug's death. It remained a hard burden to bear.

A shower of water droplets raining down on Steve's bare

torso jolted him back abruptly to the present. Mel was standing over him, flicking her wet hair back with a wicked smile. 'Wakey, wakey.'

'That wasn't very nice.'

'I'm not a "nice" girl. I thought you knew that.'

Steve reached out and grabbed her around the back of the knees, so that she lost her balance and toppled neatly on top of him on the lounger.

'Well, I'm not a nice man, so that makes two of us.' He locked his arms around her waist.

'Oh, I think you are really, underneath that arrogant, infuriating exterior.' She smiled down into his eyes.

'Maybe,' he said, pulling her head down to his lips. 'Maybe not.'

EPILOGUE

'You can have a day-old copy of *The Times*, or a two-day-old copy of the *Sun* – someone left it on a seat over there. Which do you want?' Mel asked, standing in front of Steve.

'I'll have both. I see you've got enough to keep you occupied.'

Mel sat down beside him, hugging an armful of glossy magazines, one of them with a free novel taped to the cover. 'We don't know how long the flight's been delayed for, do we? I can't stand having nothing to read.' She squinted up at a screen suspended nearby. 'Still no gate number.'

Steve shook out a newspaper. 'Don't hold your breath. They made an announcement when you were gone. Could be another hour.'

'Great.' She started to flick through *Cosmopolitan*. '"Fifty Ways to Keep Your Lover".'

'I thought it was "Fifty Ways to Leave Your Lover"?'

'That'll be Delilah's song, then. I still can't believe she had the nerve to pull that off.' Mel rested the magazine on her lap. 'I wonder if she's happy? It must be a bit of a culture shock, in more ways than one.'

'She's got more chance of being happy with almost anyone than her husband.'

'I suppose you're right.'

'I got the impression it had been going on for some time. They seemed pretty familiar.'

'You mean, she was just waiting for someone to give her a little push?'

Steve's lips twitched. 'Something like that.'

'Did she say how they met? Somehow, I can't see Delilah hanging out with the local fishermen.'

'He's a part-time barman at the seafood place she took me to in Runaway Bay – does the evening shift. She got him doing casual shifts for Taylor, too. He was working on the yacht the other night.'

'Aah.'

'Aah?'

'They were making out on the dance floor, shocking the

ex-pats,' Mel giggled. 'Desmond will be even more pissed off when he finds out she's been carrying on with him under his nose.'

'No more than he did with Sophie.'

'Sophie?' Mel looked at him curiously. 'How do you know about Sophie?'

Steve's spine stiffened, but his expression remained unaltered. 'Taylor introduced us, at the party. How do *you* know about her?'

'She introduced herself, when I was waiting for you at the Plantation Bar, that night Taylor thumped you. Talking of which ... ' she examined his face closely, 'Dolly's poultices have done a really good job. Your eye looks fine now. What with the tan, no-one back home will ever know.'

'Just as well, it would spoil my street cred.' He yawned, stretching his arms above his head. 'What did Sophie have to say?' he asked casually.

'Bragging and bitching, mainly. She's a right cow, isn't she? I reckon those two deserve each other.'

'You're behind the times – he's given her the boot. He had a French girl on his arm yesterday.' Steve got up, checking his watch. 'I'm falling asleep here. Want a coffee?'

'OK.'

Mel waited until Steve was out of sight, and then got up, walking casually after him. Loitering behind a pillar, she watched him punch up a number on his mobile. The conversation was brief and, apparently, businesslike – she was too far away to hear what was being said – and then he snapped the phone shut and went on to a coffee stand. Mel slipped back to her seat, looking thoughtful.

Steve returned with two steaming cups of Blue Mountain coffee. 'Last chance to taste the genuine article.'

'No, it's not. I've got two packs of beans in my bag.' She took the cup. 'Just think, in another ten hours or so, we'll be back to normal. Albert Square, the Vic, E20 – it'll be like we've never been away.'

'Some things will have changed.'

'How do you know?' She threw a suspicious glance at him.

Steve shrugged. 'They always do.'

She thought about this. 'I know what you mean. It's like,

while you're on holiday, you're in this other world, and that's all that exists. You sort of think time stands still back home, but it doesn't.'

'Yeah. There'll be a ton of bills for the wedding on the mat, for a start.'

'We can pay them. We're rich.'

'Says who?'

'The way you've been flinging money round in that casino, we must be. Any man who can afford to lose that much and still come out smiling has got to be loaded.'

'Easy come. Easy go.'

She narrowed her eyes. 'Just how easily did £100,000 come, Steve?'

He put down his cup with a clatter. 'It was nothing like that amount! What do you take me for?'

'Sometimes, Steve, I just don't know.'

'Where did you get that figure from? Did Sophie say something?'

Mel got up and walked over to the window. A British Airways 747 had just landed and was taxiing slowly towards the terminal building. She sensed Steve beside her but ignored him.

'That looks like our plane,' he said.

Sighing, she picked up a strand of hair and chewed the ends, turning away from him.

'Mel.' He put a hand on her shoulder.

'Take your hand off me,' she hissed.

'She didn't tell me anything. I wish she had, now. You've obviously got something to hide.'

'So where did you get a hundred grand from? You didn't pluck that out of thin air.'

'I found it on a piece of paper in your pocket – when I was looking for my sunglasses,' she added quickly.

'And from that you're assuming...?'

'My imagination's been working overtime, Steve, ever since you started laying crazy bets in that casino.'

'OK.' He took a deep breath. 'Now look at me. I'm gonna tell you the truth, and it's nothing to get worked up about. Really.'

Mel stared at him, trying to decode his crinkly eyes. 'Go on.'

'I did some business with Desmond Taylor that came off

well. That's why I've been flush. Nothing sinister. I thought I was gonna really clean up – it looked like it was worth a hundred grand, to start with. But the deal changed, and, although I made a profit, it was a much smaller one than I originally thought it was gonna be.'

'Illegal business?'

'Keep your voice down. No. Well, not exactly.' He clocked her disbelieving expression. 'All right, yes, it was slightly dodgy. That's why I didn't want Sophie shooting her mouth off. I knew you'd get upset.'

Mel felt her eyes welling up with angry tears. This was how it was going to be with Steve, she knew that now. He would always keep a part of himself separate, there would always be 'business' that he wouldn't tell her about. Could she live with that? And how far was she compromising herself if she did?

'Mel?' he asked, concerned, reading the doubt on her face.

She turned back to stare at the tarmac, at the busload of new arrivals being ferried to the airport building, remembering the heady combination of heat and excitement that had engulfed her only a fortnight earlier. She seemed to have been through a lot since then – since the wedding day itself, in fact, with all its dramas over Phil. They had all that to face when they got home, she thought, feeling her stomach lurch. Just how Steve was going to 'deal' with Phil was not a subject they had discussed. Mel suspected this was something else he wouldn't be including her in.

'Mel. Say something. *Please*.' Steve's voice sounded almost panicky.

'I've known you for over two years,' she answered slowly, 'and I realize now I've only just scratched the surface of Steve Owen.' She looked over her shoulder at him. 'Are you ever going to let me in? I mean, properly?'

'Mel.' He put his arms around her from behind, burying his face in her hair. 'In the past two weeks I've told you more about myself than I've ever confided to anyone in my entire life. Doesn't that tell you something?'

'I – I suppose so.'

'Do you know why I married you?'

'Why?'

'Not just because you're beautiful and sexy – that goes

without saying – but because of your courage. And because of your conscience. Because you complete me. You make me a better person.' He squeezed her tightly. 'I know that might be difficult to believe, at times, but it's the truth.' She turned to him, moved. 'I know I've got a way to go,' he continued, cupping her face in his hands. 'And it won't be plain sailing, I'll tell you that now. But I'm in this for the long haul, Mel, because I need you. And because I love you.'

Mel remembered the night when she thought that he'd drowned; the sense that her life, having just found definition, had suddenly lost all substance and structure. A life without Steve was impossible to imagine. But a life with Steve – what was that going to hold?

'I know what you're thinking,' he whispered. 'But when the chips are down, you've just got to trust me. That's what this is all about. So what's it gonna be?'

Mel swallowed. 'You're my lawful wedded husband, Steve. Emphasis on the "lawful". Make sure it stays that way.'

Cast members who appear in the photographs:

Steve Owen Martin Kemp
Beppe di Marco Michael Greco
Billy Mitchell Perry Fenwick
Jackie Owen Race Davies
Gianni di Marco Marc Bannerman
Barbara Owen Sheila Hancock
Matthew Rose Joe Absolom
Saskia Duncan Deborah Sheridan-Taylor
Mark Fowler Todd Carty
Melanie Owen (née Healy) Tamzin Outhwaite
Dan Sullivan Craig Fairbrass
Lisa Shaw Lucy Benjamin
Phil Mitchell Steve McFadden